# The HOUSE on KYVERDALE ROAD

CHAIKY HALPERN

# The HOUSE on KYVERDALE ROAD

FELDHEIM PUBLISHERS
JERUSALEM   NEW YORK

*First published 1995*

Paperback: ISBN 978-0-87306-738-6

Copyright © 1995, 2023 by Chaiky Halpern

All rights reserved.
No part of this publication may be translated,
reproduced, stored in a retrieval system or
transmitted, in any form or by any means,
electronic or otherwise, even for personal use,
without written permission from the publishers.

FELDHEIM PUBLISHERS
POB 34549
Jerusalem, Israel

208 Airport Executive Park
Nanuet, NY 10954
www.feldheim.com

| Distributed in Europe by: | Distributed in Australia by: |
|---|---|
| LEHMANNS | GOLDS WORLD OF JUDAICA |
| +44-0-191-430-0333 | +613 95278775 |
| info@lehmanns.co.uk | info@golds.com.au |
| www.lehmanns.co.uk | www.golds.com.au |

Typesetting/Layout: Astronel

*Printed in USA*

*To my father* ז״ל
*whose travels gave him many opportunities
to play a role in*
והשיב לב אבות על בנים, ולב בנים על אבותם

*There really is a street named Kyverdale Road, as anyone who lives in Stamford Hill can tell you; there are records of Jewish families living there as far back as the 1860s. The characters in this book, however, are all imaginary, and any similarity to a past or present personality is purely coincidental.*

# Acknowledgments

WHEN A BOOK SPROUTS from a tiny germ of an idea and grows over a number of years, so many people play a part in bringing it to fruition that it's impossible to name each individually, let alone thank them. Such a list would include my daughter's geography teacher who gave her the first comparative ordinance survey maps detailing the differences between Stamford Hill of the nineteenth century and Stamford Hill today. It would also include the taxi driver who made me feel that I'd more or less gotten it right. (He told me that his grandparents had come to Stamford Hill from the East End and brought along their "books" from Kiev. Today he lives in Ilford, but his daughter is married to a rabbi in Jerusalem. He's given her his grandparents' "books"; she is, after all, the only member of the family who can read them.)

Nevertheless, I must thank those who head my list; without them this book would never been written:

Rabbi Michael Bernstein, whose book *The Jews of Stamford Hill* supplied me with important information;

Mr. Kahan, librarian of Jews College, who provided research material and unearthed the fascinating and fearful old issues of *Darkest Russia* and *The Jewish Chronicle*;

Rabbi and Mrs. Y. Goldman, for reading the manuscript and offering their valuable comments and suggestions; and

Esther Ostreich, for her ideas and information.

My greatest thanks are due to my family, who put up with a lot of neglect during the research and actual writing of the book. I am deeply indebted to my father-in-law, Rabbi Alter Halpern, whose expertise in every subject under the sun (and above it) goes hand in hand with his infinite patience in answering questions.

I would like to express my gratitude to Mr. Yaakov Feldheim for his longstanding encouragement, and to the members of his editorial and design departments, Dvora Rhein, Ruchi Koval, Bracha Steinberg and Harvey Klineman, who contributed to the production of this book. Last but not least, I would like to thank Feldheim's editor-in-chief, Marsi Tabak, for her expert hand, not in wielding a heavy blue pencil, but in guiding mine so that the original manuscript could grow into a book.

CHAPTER ONE

The first Sunday of every month always brought Great-Uncle Martin down to the sea for the day. Judy never paid much attention to the old man's visits; a polite hello and goodbye when he came and went was about all the conversation there had been between them for years. When she was small she watched with a fascinated eye as he gulped his coffee piping hot, and wondered if he would exhale the steam. That was all he needed to fortify himself, before he would make his way through the overgrown field that backed their garden along the worn path that marked the way to the sea.

Occasionally, Judy would catch a glimpse of him from her bedroom window which looked out onto the pebbled beach: a small upright figure dressed in faded black, perched on the two-legged stool that folded out of his walking stick. He looked to all the world like a spry old crow on the limb of a winter tree, staring out to sea.

Then, one day, out of the blue, he brought her the brooch — the one with the Hebrew lettering.

That Sunday morning had started out cold and rainy. By eleven, the sun was beginning to peep out blearily from under its cloudy cover, but that did not make much difference to Judy. She missed her daily walk along the sea, but she was still feeling quivery and weak all over from a two-week bout of flu. The wind that whipped the autumn leaves onto their sprawling lawn made her shiver and stifled any temptation she may have had to take her first step outdoors. Somehow, even her wrinkled bedcovers looked more inviting and she wondered if she should just go back to sleep. Judy eyed her room with distaste. It was littered with the debris of two weeks of enforced idleness; crumpled tissues and unfinished mugs of cocoa adorned the dresser and night table, and crossword puzzle books were scattered across the carpet.

Why don't you clear up this wreck? Judy prodded herself. Then her stomach rumbled noisily, reminding her that she'd only picked at her breakfast that morning, so she decided to try to appease it with a cup of tea downstairs. Pausing uncertainly on the landing outside her room, she could hear the clatter of cups and saucers from the kitchen, and her uncle's wheezy chuckle floated upstairs as if carried aloft by the fragrant cloud of hot coffee. He hasn't gone down to the beach yet, thought Judy. I'm not in the mood to be friendly right now. She turned back to her bedroom door but the sound of her name made her stop, her hand still on the doorknob.

Judith. He always called her that, even when she was small enough to shrilly insist that her name was Judy.

"I've brought it for Judith," he was saying. "I've always wanted her to have it."

She could hear her mother laugh. "You don't expect her to wear it, do you, Uncle Martin?"

Another wheezy chuckle floated up the steep cottage steps. "I suppose not. But I've always wanted Judith to have it anyway."

Judy poked her head cautiously over the railing, curiosity overcoming her get-back-into-bed mood. What

## Chapter One

could Great-Uncle Martin possibly have brought her? she wondered. For a moment, wild images flashed across her mind, of going off to school dressed in a long billowing dress with a bustle, nineteenth-century style, or sauntering along the beach in a long feather boa from the roaring twenties. She stifled a giggle. Her mother, sharp-eared as ever, peered out of the kitchen door and called, "Judy? Is that you? Come on downstairs. Uncle Martin wants to say hello."

Uncle Martin looked up as Judy entered the warm fragrant kichen. She gave him her usual perfunctory smile and polite hello, while her eyes traveled down to the small oblong box that sat on the table beside his coffee cup. It was an old wooden box in a dark rusty black color with bits of beige glimmering through. The top and the bottom parts of the old-fashioned jewelry box now lay open, side by side on the table, held together by small metal hinges. Yellowing bits of tissue paper emerged from its depths.

Uncle Martin smiled. "I've finally brought this for you, Judith," he said. "Told your mum about it ages ago but I thought I'd wait until you were old enough not to laugh. At sixteen, you might like owning something without actually wearing it. Here, take a look."

Judy reached out to take whatever it was that he was holding. For a moment though, she stared at the old man's face. That was the longest stretch of words that he'd ever said to her and she was surprised to see the emotion that lurked in his eyes behind the fixed, determined smile. Then she looked down at the bit of jewelry in her hand. It was a three-inch-long oblong bar pin made of heavy silver, the type worn by ladies long ago, just below their high ruff collars. Not quite a taffeta dress with a bustle, but surely a suitable accessory for one. Judy could readily picture the beautifully engraved brooch perched above a long row of glittering jet buttons marching down the front of a severe black dress, pinched at the waist, swirling out at the ankles. But whose dress?

She looked up to find her great-uncle's eyes, surprisingly clear for a man in his eighties, resting upon her, a curious expression on his face.

"Well?"

Judy didn't quite know what to answer. "I...I guess I should say thank you very much. But...Why me? You did say you wanted me to have it, didn't you?"

"Yes, I did," Uncle Martin answered. "Well, why don't you look at the name?"

"The name?" Judy stared at him blankly and then looked down at the intricate pattern etched into the metal bar. She could make out the faint outline of what appeared to be a pair of hands above a sea of loops and whirls. Then the swirling lines and circles suddenly resolved themselves into definite shapes and she could discern two small hook-shaped figures, one in the middle and one at the end of the line. She looked up at her uncle. "Are these some sort of letters?"

Uncle Martin snorted. "You haven't taught her much," he said wryly, turning to her mother. "Not even to read a little?"

Her mother's cheeks burned red as her chin came up defensively. "What on earth does she need all that for, out here in this town?" Mrs. Marks replied, trying to keep the belligerence out of her voice. "Read what? Something she'll never see? Something she'll observe as little as you do?"

Judy was astounded to see a crimson blush slowly cover the old man's face as his eyes shifted in embarrassment. He hemmed and hawed to cover the awkward

## Chapter One

silence that suddenly chilled the kitchen.

"Well, Shirley," he finally responded, "you've got a point there. But still, not even to recognize the alphabet?"

Judy put the bar pin down in front of her great-uncle, her face alive with curiosity. "Is it Hebrew?" she asked. "What does it say?"

Uncle Martin picked up the brooch and slowly traced the pattern with his gnarled finger. Then he reached into his pocket and withdrew an old-fashioned fountain pen, the type Judy had been forced to do her handwriting exercises with back in Junior 3. Judy watched with fascination as the old man carefully scratched six spidery shapes onto the back of an old envelope. He started with the hook she had noticed at the end of the line and copied the tracing right to left.

"There you are," he finally said with a flourish. "Behold the letters of your name! Or rather — the Hebrew original: *Yehudis*."

"*Yehudis*." Judy felt the strange syllables swirl pleasurably over her tongue. "Who was she?"

Uncle Martin smiled in satisfaction. "My grandmother. And your great-great grandmother! Thought you might like to have this. You have the same name. Yehudis is Judith, you know." He eyed Judy's mother curiously. "What made you give the child that name, Shirley? I've always wondered."

Mrs. Marks laughed softly. "You won't believe this, but Granny Vi made me promise I would."

"Granny Vi! My mother?" Uncle Martin looked astonished. "When was that?"

"Oh, I was only twelve at the time. She started out one day, patiently trying to explain to me that twelve was an important birthday for me, but she gave up somewhere in the middle. And finished off in her own imperious way —

she always was an old Tartar, wasn't she? I was frankly petrified of her, old as she was."

The two adults laughed.

"So was I," Uncle Martin admitted. "But you know, she did have her softer side. I loved to watch her as she lit the candles each week. She looked warm and gentle then. Sometimes she even cried."

"Really?" Judy's mother was astonished. "She lit candles every week?"

Uncle Martin looked surprised. "Of course she did. So did my sister — your Granny Bess. Every week. No sense in lighting them now and again, is there, Shirley?" he teased.

She blushed and began to rub an imaginary stain on her sleeve. "I suppose not," she admitted. "My mother lit every Friday night that we ate together as a family. And so do I. But that doesn't happen very often, I must confess."

They were quiet for a moment while the clock ticked steadily in the warm fragrant kitchen.

"So she made you promise," Uncle Martin prompted her to continue. "Promise what?"

Judy's mother smiled, remembering. "'If you ever have a daughter,'" she quoted, "'promise me you'll name her Judith.'" She laughed. "I somehow got up the nerve to ask Grandma why but she just waved her hand impatiently. 'Never you mind why,' she said. 'Just promise me.' So I did. And then she looked at me and said, 'Judith means *Daughter of the Jewish People*. You know that, don't you?' I nodded my head dutifully even though I didn't. That was the last time I saw her; she died two weeks later. But I did keep my promise."

She looked at Judy affectionately. "You don't mind, do you?"

Judy shook her head absently; she was still examining

## Chapter One

the silver bar. "What about the hands?" she asked.

"The hands?" This time her uncle wore a blank look and he took the bit of silver to examine it again. "Oh yes! The hands. See their position? I believe that's the way the *kohen* — er, the priest — holds his hands when he blesses the people." His brow furrowed as he seemed to see the brooch for the very first time. "Now, I wonder what those hands are doing there. I never really noticed them."

Finally he shrugged his shoulders. "Don't know much about this pin, actually," he admitted. "My mother got it from her mother. I vaguely remember seeing my grandmother only once, when I was a very little lad."

Judy blinked. "Really? Where did she live?"

Uncle Martin smiled gently, remembering. "She lived up in North London. In a house on Kyverdale Road."

Uncle Martin's visits continued like clockwork — the first Sunday of each month he would come down to the sea. But ever since the day that he brought her the brooch, Judy no longer tried to avoid him. She was nearly eighteen now and she considered herself mature enough to appreciate the visits of her elderly uncle.

The morning had started out cold and blustery, but Judy bundled up and went out to brave the November wind. She walked along the sea wall down to the Bill, the outermost point on the promontory, where the land poked a long spindly finger out into the sea. From here the shore receded on either side; on a clear night, you could see the lights of Portsmouth, miles down along the coast. Today, thick gray clouds scudded across the leaden skies, obscuring the horizon, drawing along behind them a thick gray mist that shrouded the sky and sea and melted the two together.

Her feet automatically went their usual route, and

although every step drew her nearer to the spot where Great-Uncle Martin was sitting, Judy did not change direction. She had not spoken much to him since that conversation at the kitchen table when he had brought her the silver brooch, but her stay-out-of-his-way attitude had long disappeared. Besides, he had picked a perfect spot for this weather; the bank of pebbles and shells that marked summer high tide level provided some shelter from the wind.

Great-Uncle Martin smiled at her from his perch above the sand. "Take a seat," he invited, pointing to the nearest boulder. "Make yourself at home."

Judy laughed as she complied. For a while, the old man and the girl sat in companionable silence, watching the surf crash onto the shore. Each foam-drenched wave tried to outreach the other as the tide brought the sea gradually closer to the spot where the two were sitting.

"Won't be long till it reaches us," Uncle Martin said at last. "Time to move on."

"I suppose so," Judy answered reluctantly. "I've got stacks of homework waiting for me. I should be getting back anyway."

The old man smiled down at her sympathetically. "Lots of work, isn't it? Last year of school?"

"No, I'm staying on for sixth form," Judy answered. "But it is a lot of work. GCSE's, you know."

"Afraid I'm a bit out of it," Uncle Martin admitted. "Tell me about it."

Judy eyed her uncle curiously, surprised at his apparent interest in her studies. "I'm trying hard for at least three A's," she heard herself tell him. "Then come A levels. If I do the same then, I hope I get my first preference in University choice. There's really only one place I want to get into."

## Chapter One

"Where's that?"

"Winchester University College," Judy answered in a sudden rush. "They've got the best Journalism course around and I simply must do it."

Uncle Martin's smile was not patronizing, just friendly. "Oh, is that what you're planning? Feel you're cut out to be a reporter?"

Judy laughed ruefully. "I think I've got an inquiring mind. Mum calls it just plain nosy."

The old man chuckled. "Isn't it always like that?" he asked. "You know, I'm the one who has a healthy ego, is steadfast and strong-minded while the other fellow is the one who is arrogant, obstinate, aggressive and pushy!"

They both laughed.

"So what are you so busy with right now?"

"It's my Geography project," Judy confided. "I've got a great idea that could really land me an A. Problem is, I can't decide how to actually do it." She poured some pebbles between her fingers reflectively. "Mum won't let me stay in a Bed-and-Breakfast in the middle of London. Even if Penny comes with me like she said she would. Mum says it's too dangerous. So how do I write up a project about Inner City life without actually experiencing it? Isn't that what a good reporter does?"

"I'm not sure I follow you." Uncle Martin said carefully. "You've got to do some sort of project on the Inner City, you say. Company isn't the problem, I take it; you've got a friend to come with you."

Judy nodded. "Penny and I have always been friends even though she is older. She's finished school already and is working in her father's shop. But it's slow season now so he won't mind her taking a break and coming along to London. She says she'd love to do some shopping at the sales there."

"So what's the problem? You need a fairly decent place to stay?"

Judy nodded again. "Just somewhere to sleep and observe the natives, you know."

Uncle Martin laughed. "The natives, you say. Well, I happen to own a place in what you might call an Inner City area. It's about to be renovated after the last tenant, but the electricity is still on and I even think the telephone's in working order. Sound good?"

"Sounds great!" Judy beamed. "Where is it?"

"I think I've mentioned it to you before," Uncle Martin said, smiling. "It's the old house on Kyverdale Road."

CHAPTER TWO

It was morning on Kyverdale Road and the orange sun shone in at an odd angle through the split in the board that covered the window, bouncing off the stack of old brittle newspapers in the corner. Judy scuffed at the yellowing heap with her sneaker, and watched a bold black headline crumble into nothingness at the touch of her toe. She prodded the pile with her broom, searching for hidden treasures, then sneezed as a cloud of dust billowed up from the bristles and fanned out across the room. Judy idly followed its path as it rose up past the skirting boads, drifting past the ornate mantlepiece as it poked spindly smoky fingers along the narrow ledge that hugged the height of the walls.

Looking up at the high gray ceiling stretched above her, Judy suddenly shivered. The lone bare lightbulb that hung at the center seemed all at once to loom above her from a great height. There was something about this room, she mused. It was not just that the old Victorian ceiling was about as high as the second floor of their modern seaside cottage back home. There was a definite atmosphere that filled it as surely as the dust she'd just kicked up.

"Psst! Judy, open up! It's me!"

Judy jumped and her broom clattered down into the floorboards, sending an old soda bottle skittering noisily across the empty room. Another sneeze shook her as she padded over to the front door and a faint giggle floated through the waggling lid of the postal slot.

"Judy? Hay fever in December?"

"Shh!" Judy shook her head at the pale blue eyes peering through the metal slit in the door. "Anybody around, Penny? Or do you want to come through the board?"

"I'll leave that to you, thank you!" Penny's eyes grew round with apprehension and she turned to look up and down the road. "All safe," she hissed dramatically.

Judy wrestled with the rusted lock, then pulled the door open just wide enough for her friend to squeeze through. "Quick!" she urged.

Penny backed into the narrow hallway, the hood of her bulky purple anorak jacket entering the house before her, an armload of groceries behind. The door clicked shut and the two girls listened for any signs of life outside that might betray a nosy neighbor.

"Seems alright," Judy whispered. She jumped again as a packet of biscuits slipped out of the overflowing grocery bag and thudded onto the floor.

"Ooh! You are jumpy today, Judy." Penny stifled a giggle. Then she frowned. "You know, this is crazy. I thought you *want* the neighbors to see you."

Judy bent to pick up the biscuits. "Well, you're the one who didn't want to come through the boarded window. And we can't exactly let them see we've got keys to the house, can we?"

"Guess not," Penny shrugged. "But it's your project, Ju, so I'll leave the climbing to you."

She hauled her heavy carrier bag down the three sag-

## Chapter Two

ging hallway steps to the kitchen. "Let's get unloaded now."

Judy nodded absently, eyeing the bright red cellophane on the biscuit package. "What are these, anyway?"

"I don't know." Penny shrugged. "Ginger snaps? Custard cremes? I asked the fellow for biscuits and that's what he gave me. I'm not very particular. Are you?" She peered at the strange lettering on the wrapping. "Hey! What kind of writing is that? Chinese?"

"Actually," Judy said, slowly turning the packet over in her hand. "I think it's Hebrew."

Funny. It was Hebrew lettering that had brought her to this house in the first place, Judy thought as she absently bit into a biscuit. She held her cup out for the welcome hot flow from the electric kettle. At least the electricity *was* on, as Uncle Martin had assured her it would be. She felt a momentary pang of guilt for doubting him.

The old kitchen cupboards creaked and protested as Penny unloaded her purchases onto their sagging shelves. "There, that's done," she said, dusting her hands off with housewifely efficiency. She put the milk and butter into the ancient fridge that, unbelievably, seemed to be in working order and closed it with a self-satisifed thump. Then she turned to unpack the last bag that stood on the rickety table.

Judy stared. "What on earth did you buy all that for?" she asked. The orange crate that served as a chair creaked ominously under her as she leaned forward in lively astonishment. "Planning a house-warming party or something?"

"Don't be silly," Penny said good-naturedly. "Don't you think we should have a good supply of groceries while we're here?" Putting the huge container of Rough-Tough household cleaner in a prominent position near the kitchen sink she added, "And besides, what's wrong with a little cleanliness? At least it'll give me something to do while you're busy with your project. You write and I'll clean. Okay?"

Judy laughed. "Alright with me," she said, "If that's the way you want to spend your winter holiday."

"Better than spending it on a geography project. I must admit I never did that when I was in school." Penny looked at Judy with a strange mixture of curiosity and affection. "I don't quite have your ambition, Judy Marks. Where you get it I really don't know."

Judy shrugged. "Ambition?" she said lightly. "I really wouldn't call it a fancy name like that. Just wanting to do something with myself, and get somewhere, I guess. But really, Penny. What about your shopping? I thought you wanted a break from your father's fish shop, and you said Kyverdale Road would suit you fine."

"For sure," Penny said with an exaggerated drawl. "Anything suits me fine. You know that. Old Eager-to-Please Penelope. That's me."

Judy nodded as she reflected on the past that she and Penny shared. The two girls had been friends for so long that they did everything together out of sheer habit. Ever since she could remember, they had walked home from school together, Penny dropping her off first at the wrought-iron gates that shut in their massive front lawn, before continuing further down the road to her family's small beachfront cottage. Even after Penny had finished school, two years ahead of Judy, the two girls had often enjoyed a quiet walk along the beach, or better yet, a leisurely sail in one of Penny's father's boats to try their fisherman's luck. Penny was more experienced and patient than Judy; she was content to lie back in the leaky boat for a quiet snooze or sunbath, or absent

## Chapter Two

contemplation of the sky, only sitting up with practiced ease at the slightest sign of a nibble.

Penny was a comfortable friend to be with, but lately, Judy found herself restive in her company. Her active mind would race ahead of the idly bobbing boat, as if riding a wave that finally overcame the quiet swells and reached the shore before them. Still, it had been only natural for Judy to ask Penny to come with her on her London adventure, and it had seemed appropriate for Penny to accept.

"It was really nice of you to agree to come with me, Penny," Judy finally brought out with a politeness that sat awkwardly between the two friends. "I really appreciate it."

"Don't be silly," Penny said for a second time. "When do I ever get to London? It'll be fun! Besides, December's not exactly boat weather, is it, and there's nothing much to do." She picked up the bottle of Rough-Tough and brandished it playfully at Judy. "Alright now! Where do we start?"

Judy led the way into the front room. "I don't know why, but I just love this room," she said, eyeing the rococo ceiling appreciatively. "Don't you just get a good feeling when you look at it?"

Penny looked around skeptically. "A feeling of dust and must, you mean?" She pointed to the heap of newspapers in the corner. "I see you've also been playing housewife. And here you are ribbing me."

"Now, look here," Judy began defensively.

"Hold it! Don't take offense!" Penny laughed. "I was only kidding. Seriously though, are you planning to keep the windows boarded up? Shouldn't we announce our presence to the neighbors?"

"I don't really know how to start," Judy confessed.

"What do you think? If we were real squatters, we'd have gotten in through the window somehow. Then we'd wait to see if the neighbors report us, or the council gets around to noticing us, and then, if we were settling in for a long stay, we'd change the locks and use our own keys."

"Are you going to write about all that?" Penny asked.

"It's all in the project," Judy explained. "I want to talk about life in inner city areas, you know. Not the facts and figures — more about the feelings — the psychological stuff. How much do neighbors get involved with each other? You know, twenty bottles of milk piling up on the doorstep before a neighbor realizes the fellow's had a heart attack or something. That sort of thing."

"I wonder..." Penny began. She hesitated, eyeing Judy doubtfully. "Now, don't get angry, Ju, but I wonder if you're going to get what you came for."

Judy stared. "What on earth do you mean?"

"I really don't know," Penny faltered, groping for the words to explain. "I've just been at the grocery. Now, I know this place is meant to be a city area, but it sure didn't feel like it, standing in that queue by the till. I mean, all the people waiting there seemed to know each other, like people in a small town. At least, they acted like they did."

"Do you think so?" Judy asked. She thought a moment. "Well, we'll just have to wait and see. The street seems very quiet. I know we only came today and it's not exactly playing-outside weather so we haven't seen anybody much. I've tried to peer through the crack in the board but I still don't even know who lives next door."

"Actually, I saw a girl going in there when I came down the road with the shopping," Penny said. "Don't worry," she added hastily. "She didn't see my face; I hid behind the grocery bags, and I waited until she was gone before

## Chapter Two

I called you."

"Really?" Judy wondered. "A girl our age? And there hasn't been a peep from next door all day long. Maybe these old walls are too thick to hear anything."

As if to purposely contradict her, a sudden unearthly sound emitted from the anonymous house next door. It started with a low growl which worked up into a high-pitched screech, and finally ended in a series of unnerving bumps and thuds. The two girls clutched each other soundlessly, their faces frozen into white masks of terror. Then they both laughed sheepishly at the sight of each other's expressions while the thudding noises continued to sound, harmlessly now, from behind the brick fireplace.

"Whew, we're both edgy, Judy," Penny gulped, taking a deep breath to steady herself. "Someone scrapes a chair against the floor and we nearly go through the ceiling."

"Sounds like they're setting up tables and chairs for something," Judy said shakily. "Think they're having a party?"

"Don't know," Penny shrugged. "But they could bring a brass band for all I care. We've had a long ride from Chichester today and I'm so tired I'm going to go to sleep now and I *know* I wouldn't hear a thing. Planning to make an early night too?"

"I guess so," Judy agreed. "It was an awfully late one last night what with packing and planning all the rest. I'll be ready soon to hit the sack."

Hitting the sack early didn't guarantee an early night, Judy thought ruefully as she checked her watch for the tenth time since Penny had fallen asleep. First a hard mound somewhere down by her ankles dug into her every time she tried to find a comfortable sleeping position. She tried to move a bit to the right or the left, but her feet insisted on resting on the exact location of that angular whatever-it-was sticking to the bottom of the sleeping bag. She slid her hand under the sacking to see if there was anything on the floor beneath her, but could only feel the dusty linoleum painting her palm gray. In the end, she crawled head first into the sleeping bag, feeling before her as she went, and finally discovered the culprit. So that's where her toothbrush had disappeared to!

All told, the toothbrush adventure took the better part of an hour, but even when it was over, Judy still lay awake. The upstairs windows were not boarded over, but old faded curtains screened out the streetlight that tried to filter in through the grime-encrusted windows. Judy lay on her back staring at the black shadows on the ceiling and listening in the darkness. Funny how each house has its own character and sounds, she thought. Just like each person has his very own voice different from that of everyone else. Floorboards creaked and lead pipes clanked in companionable conversation as the old house settled and vibrations from any outside traffic stopped for the night. Occasionally a quiet murmur from the house next door seemed to travel up the fireplace, penetrating the room where Judy lay, wallowing in her insomnia. She looked at her watch for the umpteenth time. It was awfully quiet next door for a party but, whatever it was, it seemed to be going on for some time. Earlier in the evening, while they had eaten their improvised supper of hot cheese toast with beans, they had heard car doors slamming as the visitors arrived. It was already past eleven now and she had yet to hear them leave. What type of people could they be? she wondered. So many of them packed into a room and yet you could hardly hear a thing. What could they be doing there?

## Chapter Two

Finally the scraping and thumping of chairs began to sound again from behind the wall, this time accompanied by the murmur of many cheerful voices. Whatever they had been doing, they seemed happy about it, Judy thought as she turned over in her sleeping bag, which was by now a sweaty and rumpled mess. She looked enviously past the fan heater, where Penny was sleeping peacefully. Car doors began to slam again and she could hear quiet voices outside, with an occasional goodbye and thanks-so-much rising above the stillness. Who were these people? Judy thought. Go on, look out the window. Better not — they'll think you're a peeping Tom. They'll go and report you and that'll be the end of your project.

Curiosity battled with caution until Judy decided to go downstairs instead and peer out through the crack in the board. She tiptoed quietly out of the dark bedroom, avoiding the worn floorboards that creaked horrendously, and padded out into the hall. The small bulb on the ceiling cast a surprisingly friendly glow all the way down to the front door. The front room door at the right stood invitingly open and a simple warmth seemed to emerge from it, drifting up the stairs where Judy stood, to envelop her in it and guide her down, even as the old linoleum felt so cold and clammy to her bare feet.

By the time she reached the window, the last car door had slammed shut and Judy could see a shadowy hand from inside the vehicle, waving cheerfully to a teenage girl standing just inside the next-door hedge. As the car drove away, the girl's smiling face was framed by the dark red glow of the departing tail lights, and then she turned back into her house. She looks nice, reflected Judy, still peering out onto the by now empty street. Even if she does dress like someone's grandmother.

The warmth that had accompanied Judy down the

hallway steps still hung comfortably about her and she suddenly felt as if a motherly hand were tapping her on the shoulder, urging her to get back into bed. She turned away from the window, her eyes still puckered from the effort of peering through the crack. The white rays of light from the streetlamp outside blinded her as she turned back to the dark empty room. She could feel the cold mist creep through the crack in the board and into her toes, right up through her, and with a sudden shiver, she raced up the stairs to the warm safe nest of her sleeping bag.

Almost immediately, Judy could feel herself falling asleep. The ceiling arched up and away from her and she felt a strange sensation of slanting downward at the toes, as if about to fall down the stairs feet first. Only this time, half her brain seemed to stay awake and she could actually see the stairs as she stood before them, hesitating as she looked down the steep incline. Her back arched as she felt herself sailing down, down, and she clutched her sleeping bag for support, waiting for the blessed blackness that signaled sleep or a sudden bump instead. Her toes curled into the quilted mound beneath her, as if frantically assuring her that she actually lay in bed, but at the same time, she could feel the cracked linoleum, cold to the touch of her feet, as she came to a gentle stop at the foot of the stairs.

*Once again, Judy stood in the hallway before the front room with the boarded up windows, only this time, the door seemed to be boarded up as well. A sudden buzzing sound filled her head and as she stood and watched, the wooden board at the doorway slowly dissolved into a misty curtain. A warm light glowed behind the swaying material, a light separate from the single bare lightbulb*

## Chapter Two

*high in the hallway ceiling. Judy reached out a tentative hand to whisk the curtain aside, but it slowly solidified into a solid barrier that barred her entry. Solid yet translucent, as if someone had poured buckets of water over the doorway, and the water had frozen into a hazy, icy mass, like frost on a windowpane. It actually felt cold to the touch of her fingertips and Judy hastily withdrew her hands, as she strained to see through it to the room beyond.*

*This was definitely the front room that she had stood and swept that day. Judy could make out the ornate ceiling, the big stone fireplace, the fine carving on the mantlepiece. But a warm glowing fire flickered now in the fireplace, secure behind a black wrought-iron grate. Dozens of china ornaments were arrayed upon the shelving, flanked by a pair of brass candlesticks polished to a rich shine. And above it all, a stately, pink-tinged mirror graced the wall, bordered on all sides by deep wine and cream striped wallpaper.*

*By now, the buzzing had stopped but the barrier was still firmly in place. Judy strained forward to see the shadowy shapes reflected in the mirror, but they grew ever fainter as the seconds ticked away. The bold stripes on the wallpaper began to melt into each other as the fire slowly died in the grate, and the light began to fade, seeping into the darkness around her until it was gone.*

*Judy took a step forward and no ice or wooden board barred her way as she stepped gingerly through the open doorway. She blinked and looked again, but there was nothing left to see. Only the peeling blue paint on the walls and the chipped plaster mantlepiece stared back at her, forlorn, in the empty room. She could feel the cold hard flooring beneath her feet growing slowly warmer and softer, and, digging her toes into the blanket around her, Judy drifted off to sleep.*

CHAPTER THREE

The next day, Judy wandered around the house like a puppy whose owners had moved away and left him alone in an empty flat. The scene that had filtered through the strange barrier in her dream last night flickered in her brain all day like some disjointed screenplay, but she could not quite recapture exactly what she'd seen. The odd part of it all was that when the light had faded and she'd found herself alone at the foot of the old steep stairway that stretched into the yawning upstairs darkness, she had never felt afraid. She felt more like someone who heard her best friend knock at the door, but when she got there and opened it, she found that her friend had gone. There was no spooky feeling of Who-knocked? or Who-was-it? but rather the disappointed feeling of Sorry-I-missed-her.

Judy's usual get-up-and-go was replaced with an odd sort of languor that she didn't know what to do with. Her mind and mood swung back and forth all day like a pendulum. One moment she was trying to remember what had happened last night, staring around the front room in a vain effort to recapture the scene, and the next, she was shaking herself impatiently, insisting that it had been, after all, only a dream. Or perhaps it was the effect of the white and red lights, and the hot cheese toast she'd had just before bedtime.

Penny, on the other hand, was feeling full of vim and vigor after a refreshingly long sleep in a snug sleeping bag, ready to tackle her self-imposed task of cleaning the house. Armed with a few oversized sponges she'd bought and the big container of Rough-Tough, by mid-morning she had shaved a few layers of soot off the carved mantlepiece and lovingly polished the jade green tiles that formed an ornate border round the fireplace. The peeling white hardboard that shut off the fireplace rattled as she worked.

"I wonder what's behind this," she said absently, dipping her sponge into the old plastic pail she'd found in the kitchen pantry. "Just imagine some old gray flagstones with a hundred-year build-up of soot and ashes."

"More like a black iron grate, I should think," Judy answered quietly. She looked at the dismal blue paint on the walls, slashed across with ever widening cracks that ran erratically across them like the lines on a graph gone berserk. "That wishy washy blue is awful," she grimaced. "Now just imagine this room with some strong character colors. How about a deep wine and cream wallpaper in nice bold stripes?"

For a moment, Penny stared at Judy. Then she laughed. "Didn't know you're going in for interior decorating, Ju," she teased. "I thought you're all set to be a reporter. But here I am slaving away and you haven't even picked up a pen."

"A pen?" Judy said in mock arrogance. "How about a microphone?" She picked up the old red floorbrush and held it before her mouth with a flourish. "Here is an on-the-scene report with Judith Marks," she said, putting her eye to the crack in the board. "The first thing I can see...Ouch!"

## Chapter Three

Judy hastily removed the offending bristles from her cheek and turned the ragged brush over, holding the handle side to her mouth instead. Penny giggled as Judy started again.

"Ahem...Excuse me, ladies and gentlemen. The first vehicle coming down this road is a three-wheeled open milk van driven by a red-headed milkman. Note the whine of its electric motor and the rattle of the milk bottles as he delivers them to the doorsteps of the houses. Note as well that not every household on this road seems to get milk deliveries. In fact it seems that at this end of the road most of them don't."

She turned around at the sound of a hearty yawn from Penny. "I beg your pardon. Am I boring you?"

"Not at all," Penny said hastily. "Go on."

"The street at present seems to be deserted," Judy intoned. "A lone woman with a shopping cart is walking along ever so slowly down this peaceful road. Across the way I think I see a little boy riding his bicycle, or is it tricycle?"

"You've got to get your details right, Judy," Penny said with mock severity.

"Alright, alright. It is a tricycle. And if you must know, he's got a blue velvet cap or something on his head and an awfully funny hairstyle and...speaking of hairstyles — there are another two funny ones coming along."

"You're not sounding very professional anymore, Ju," Penny commented, not missing a stroke of the sponge. "But at least you're getting interesting."

"No really, these two fellows in black leather jackets look like they're pretending to be Red Indians with spiky Mohawk hairstyles. All they need are a couple of machetes. Or do I mean tomahawks? Though they seem to be quite peaceful. At any rate, they're strolling along minding their own business. No. Now they're stopping. Hey! What do they think they're doing?"

The wet sponge hung suspended in midair as Penny gaped at Judy. "What's happening?"

"They've stopped near that lady and I think they're up to no good." Judy babbled. "What do I do? Ooo! They've pushed her down. Her glasses are on the ground! Ooo! He smashed them! That hoodlum!"

"Here, let me see!" Penny elbowed her way to the crack and the two girls stood cheek to cheek trying to see out.

"What do we do?"

"Should we call the police?"

"Should we go out to help her?"

"Are you mad? They'll attack us too!"

For a moment, Penny and Judy argued over the next step to take, all the time jostling for a better view. Then suddenly, the long suffering sheet of hardboard fell to the ground and they were left staring out the gaping hole in the front window, with a grandstand view of the scene in the street.

It had all taken no more than two minutes but it was like a film played in slow motion. Before their frozen gaze, the two thugs emptied the woman's shopping cart, then leaned over the prone figure on the ground, working to find the pockets of her thick coat. It was a silent film as well until a blood-curdling scream sounded from across the road:

*KHAPTZEM!*

At the sound of those strange two syllables, windows flew up and heads emerged, then doors banged open and people began to fill the street.

This time it was pure amazement, not fear, that froze the two girls to their post at the windowsill. The street became alive with people, housewives still clutching their

## Chapter Three

dishcloths, toddlers waddling after them down the front steps. A car that had been passing by braked suddenly and stopped, two bearded men emerging from either side to see what was happening.

"There they go!" yelled a little boy, abandoning his bike and dancing up and down the pavement in near hysteria, pointing to the now-fleeing figures. He seemed to enjoy the ruckus he'd caused with his single shout.

A small knot of women clustered about the elderly woman, helping her up from the ground. Judy recognized the girl from next door; she was busily collecting the scattered greens and groceries from the pavement, and putting them neatly back into the shopping cart. That snapped Judy out of her comatose state. "Look at us," she gasped to Penny. "Just standing here staring out the window. Let's see if we're needed."

"Wh-what do they need *us* f-for?" Penny stammered, but Judy was already halfway out the door.

Judy managed to retreive a few forgotten potatoes that had rolled into the street and approached the girl who was standing with the shopping cart. She seemed to be contemplating whether she should follow the crowd of women who were now entering one of the neighboring houses.

"Should I drop these in?" Judy asked shyly.

"Yes. Thanks." The other girl eyed her curiously. Then she turned to watch a blue car that was hastily parking across the road.

"Is anyone phoning for police, or first aid?" Judy asked hesitantly.

"Someone must have done that already," the girl replied pleasantly, pointing to the neatly dressed young man emerging from the car, medical bag in hand. "That's the first aid."

That evening, over yet another hot cheese toast, Judy and Penny discussed the afternoon episode.

"You know, Penny," Judy said reflectively, absently winding a long yellow strand of melted cheese around her finger. "I'm not sure a reporter is a very nice person."

Penny laughed lazily. "Having a change of heart, Ju?"

"No, really, Penny. Think about it. There you are, reporting a scene that's happening before your eyes. You're busy talking about it, taking pictures of it, sometimes of the most awful things, and you're just standing there and watching and not doing a thing!"

"Like us at the window today?"

"Yes. Like us at the window." Judy admitted ruefully. "That's what made me suddenly rush out like that. Here I am making a report on all these city dwellers who are supposedly cold and distant and uncaring, and I'm the one who stands and watches while *they* all rush out to help!"

"Was it some sort of signal that brought them out?" Penny wondered aloud. "What did that little boy shout anyway?"

"Good question," Judy shrugged. "But it must have been a code or something that made them all run out to help. Penny, the feeling that I got when I watched them all rush out together is probably the exact feeling that you got waiting in line in the grocery store. These people really do act like they know each other. I wonder what sort of report I'll be able to write in this place after all."

Could this project just be a waste of time? No! For some reason, Judy felt sure of that, even as she lay, restless again in her sleeping bag, after a long day of accomplishing absolutely nothing. Once again, Penny had gone right off to sleep by simply flinging her right arm over her eyes and POOF! she was out like a light.

## Chapter Three

And Judy lay staring into the dark, not a word of her project planned or written, but still feeling happy she'd come to this house on Kyverdale Road.

As the sounds of the street quieted down for the night, with only the distant wail of a siren disturbing the stillness outside, the flooring and plumbing began their refrain. This time, however, the chairs and tables next door seemed to be standing in their rightful places and there was no indistinct murmur traveling up the chimney. Whatever it was that they did yesterday did not seem to be repeating itself tonight.

A sudden creak below, louder than the friendly chorus of floorboards and pipes, suddenly jerked Judy into a sitting position.

What was that?

Judy sat motionless a moment, straining to hear in the stillness. A further creak, then a grating sound brought her up and out of the sleeping bag. She was halfway down the staircase before she stopped to think. Last night's noises had been friendly, and she knew just what she had gone to see. Tonight, however, all was quiet outside. The sounds definitely came from inside the house. For a moment she wondered if the strange buzzing sound would begin again, and what she would see when she entered the front room. She hesitated, then her old curiosity reasserted itself and she took the last few stairs with a single bound, purposely making noise as she went.

Immediately, the grating sound came again, followed by thumps and thuds, and the crackling of branches outside. Cautiously, Judy poked her head around the half-opened door, and was surprised to feel a chilly night breeze brush across her face. For a moment, an unaccountable disappointment filled her as she saw the bare, dusty room. Then her eyes took in the broken front window, exposed to the dark street outside, and a shadowy shape racing down the road. A shiver of fear prickled her spine as she realized there really had been someone there only a moment before.

A sudden creak on the hallway stairs set her heart pounding.

"Judy? Is that you?"

Judy felt her breath hiss out like a deflating gas balloon. "Penny? Yes. I'm here."

Penny's face peered anxiously around the front room door. "Oh! We forgot to nail the board back onto the window. Did someone try to come in?"

Judy nodded with a quavery laugh. "I guess we're not the only squatters in town," she said shakily. "I mean, it couldn't have been a burglar. There's nothing much here to take, is there?"

"Not really," Penny agreed. "Let's concentrate on putting the board back over the window somehow. Tomorrow we can try to get hold of a hammer and nails to bang it back in place."

The two girls struggled with the big plank of wood, working to position it over the long narrow window.

"That will have to do," Penny nodded as she stepped back to observe their handiwork. "Now let's go back to sleep."

She turned towards the doorway while Judy eyed the boarded window doutfully.

"Whoops! There it goes!"

With a majestic forward sweep, the board fell gracefully from its perch before the broken window and landed on the floor with a crash that reverberated throughout the house. As if for an encore, the peeling bit of hardboard fell out of the fireplace, displaying in all its glory a black wrought-iron grate, covered in soot and grime.

## Chapter Three

"Do you see that, Judy?" Penny whispered.

Judy nodded, then blinked as she followed Penny's upward gaze. The double crash had widened the crack in the plastered wall, and a triangular sheet of pale blue paint had slipped to the floor, revealing a patch of the old-fashioned wall covering that had once decorated the room. It was faded and shabby but the colors were unmistakable: deep wine and light cream in a strong bold stripe.

CHAPTER FOUR

"Honestly, Penny," Judy sighed for the tenth time that morning. "I don't know why I said it. Cream and wine just sounded right. That's all."

She took a careful sip of her hot tea and looked up to see Penny eyeing her doubtfully. The steaming liquid sloshed onto the table as she set the cup down hard. "And we'd better not have cheese toast tonight, you hear?"

Penny blinked. "What on earth does that have to do with it?"

"Nothing," Judy muttered, taking another sip.

Penny sat quietly, munching her toast, her eyes on Judy's pale face. "You know, Judy," she finally said. "I think this place is getting to us. We've been sitting holed up in the house since we arrived; if not for those two punks yesterday, we wouldn't have poked our noses outside all day long. And you haven't even gotten any writing done, have you?" She didn't wait for Judy's reply but rattled on.

"Let's get out a bit, Judy. The neighbors have seen us already. I'm sure of that. So you can write about them pretending not to see you, or something. We can go up to the main road and explore a bit, or even get on a bus and do some touring. Have you ever been to Madame

Tussaud's Wax Museum?"

Judy looked interested yet hesitant. "We'd better do something about that window first, don't you think? I'm not in the mood for any more visitors tonight."

"Well, you did say it's an inner city area," Penny pointed out teasingly. "By day a mugging, by night an intruder. You know, I'll be glad to get home in one piece."

After a day of touring, it was growing dark by the time the two girls returned to their stop at the intersection in the main road of Stamford Hill. The street and storefront lights decorated the frosty roads like hundreds of birthday candles on white icing. The big red bus swung away, disappearing into the rush hour traffic.

"Good thing we bought that travel card," Penny commented as she crumpled the well-worn bit of cardboard in her hand. "We've been hopping on and off buses all day long, all for the price of the card."

"That was a good idea of yours to take the Number 13 down Baker Street," Judy agreed. "Now we can actually say we've been to Selfridge's. They say the Queen shops there, you know." She laughed. "And it was fun, even if all we did was hang around outside looking at the holiday displays."

"Beauty and the Beast," Penny smiled. "Isn't it unbelievable how they turn those display windows into theater settings? I think they attract even more attention than their usual well-dressed mannequins! My cousin Joan was in London last year around this time and she went to see the West End lights. Selfridge's had an Alice in Wonderland display that year, with fantastic cardboard people that looked so real!"

As they turned off the main road, away from the shine of the shop lights, Judy shivered. "Awfully dark around here, isn't it," she mused. "None of the usual December

## Chapter Four

strings of lights."

"Not even in the shop windows," Penny added. "None of the tinsel and stuff strung from the traffic lights. I wonder why."

They crossed the road quickly before distant pinpricks of lights could grow into oncoming headlamps. Penny watched with satisfaction as Judy bounded along beside her all the way home with the old spring back in her step. The day out had done them good, she reflected. Nothing like a good airing out to shake the cobwebs from your brain.

"That was fun, wasn't it?" Judy smiled at her as they walked along down the darkening street. "But you never did get a souvenir, did you?"

They both laughed, remembering. The lady at the souvenir till in Madame Tussaud's had seemed very busy with something, absolutely ignoring them as they tried to catch her attention.

"I beg your pardon," Judy mimicked. "I beg...er..um.."

"And I was so polite!" Penny guffawed. "It was only when I looked down at what she was so busy with that I realized she was made of wax!"

They were still laughing when they turned onto Kyverdale Road. The tall trees lining the street swayed in the wind, their branches throwing shadows across the road as they played with the lights of the streetlamps. Penny tightened her anorak hood and shivered as a sudden gust of wind sailed around the corner. "Brr. It's cold. Good thing your Mum called before we left and told you how to get the heating going. That fan heater wouldn't be much good in this weather."

There was no reply from Judy, and Penny looked up to see her staring down the road at their house.

"What's up?" she asked.

"The window. That's what." Judy replied shortly. Instinctively, she broke into a run, and Penny followed. A brand new window glinted where the board had been and white blinds covered both front windows from prying eyes.

"What on earth…"

The two girls stood staring at the front of the house, wondering if they dared to go in. It actually looked lived in now, even though it seemed dark and silent inside. A soft footfall sounded behind them and they both turned with one movement, like two clockwork soldiers wound up to go.

"Oh, hello." Judy laughed nervously as she recognized the girl from next door. Judy hadn't noticed how tall she was; she found herself looking upward in order to meet her eyes.

The girl stopped and smiled. "Hello," she said quietly, looking at the shining new windowpane. "Happy with your home improvements?"

The two girls stared. "Our what?"

For a moment the girl looked puzzled, then her face cleared. "Oh, sorry. I didn't realize you haven't been inside yet. Bill has been banging around there all day today. Actually, I never did see him leave."

She turned around to check the cars parked at the curb.

"Yes, that's his old jalopy over there," she said, pointing to a dusty red mini-van with ladder hooks on its roof. "He's probably still inside. Said the landlord wanted it done for you."

Judy blinked. "For us? Who's Bill?"

"Bill's a handyman who lives around the corner. He always does work in this neighborhood. Said your uncle called him to do the job." She hesitated. "It is your uncle

## Chapter Four

who owns this place, isn't it? You aren't squatters or something, are you?"

Judy and Penny exchanged sheepish smiles as they thought of all the time they'd spent peering through the crack in the board. "No, of course not," Judy hastily denied as she fumbled for the door key. "It is my uncle. Actually, my great-great-uncle, I think. How did you know he owns it?"

"Well, you usually know something about the house next door to you, don't you?" The girl shrugged. "I think my father knows him." She looked at the two girls curiously and seemed to want to say something else, then changed her mind.

Just then her front door opened and a soft voice called quietly, "Malka, are you there?"

"Here, Mummy. Coming right in." She turned apologetically to the two girls. "Sorry. I'd better go in now. They'll be needing my help setting up." A familiar series of thumps and thuds sounded through the open front door, echoing across the quiet street.

"Are you having another party?" Judy asked curiously.

"Another what?" the girl stared at Judy for a moment. Then she laughed. "Oh, did we disturb you the other night? No, it's not a party. It's a series of lectures that my father gives. We have quite a crowd now that it's the winter holidays."

"Lectures? What sort of lectures?"

Malka hesitated, then decided Judy was being friendly. "Lectures on Jewish topics," she explained. "They're for beginners in Judaism."

"Oh, that's nice," Judy said for lack of anything better to say. "That sounds...er...interesting." She turned to follow Penny up the path to their front door, then for some reason that she could not quite explain, she found herself stopping, looking back at Malka's pleasant face. "I'm Jewish too, you know," she offered, then wondered why she'd said it. "My name is Judith. Judith Marks."

Malka didn't miss a beat. "I thought you might be Jewish," she said matter-of-factly. "I know your uncle is. Or is it great-great?"

The two girls laughed, some of the awkwardness between them falling away. Malka turned to go, then she looked back at Judy. "Want to join us tonight?" she asked, deliberately offhand.

Judy was taken aback. "Oh no. No. I mean, no, thank you. That's very...um...very nice of you, but I'd feel foolish. I mean..."

She stopped in confusion, not sure if she'd stepped on any toes, but Malka just laughed again. It was a very nice, tinkly laugh, Judy thought suddenly. Very natural, not at all false and put on.

"That's alright," Malka said good naturedly. "It's not by invitation only. Anyone can come. But if you think you need some excuse, you're a neighbor, you know. You can always knock on the door to borrow some sugar and then stay to listen!" Her tinkly laugh drifted over her shoulder as she turned to go, and with a friendly wave, she disappeared into her house.

Judy caught up with Penny on the front doorstep where Penny was standing, her ear to the door. "I don't think anyone's inside," Penny said in a whisper. "I've knocked a couple of times and I don't hear a thing."

Judy shrugged. "Well, we do have keys."

For a moment, the two girls wrestled with the rusted lock. At least this time, they didn't have to battle in secretive silence.

When the house finally admitted them, they hesitated a moment before entering. The unexpected window blinds

## Chapter Four

had unnerved them more than they'd cared to admit and when they finally stepped inside they tiptoed, like someone entering a hotel room that he was almost sure wasn't his.

"What did you expect to see?" Penny laughed as Judy peered cautiously into the front room. "A fire in the grate and someone rocking on a chair in front of it?"

The empty room looked reassuringly as they had left it, except that the hardboard had been put back over the fireplace and clean white blinds hung where the board had been. The girls stood in the empty hallway listening.

"This Bill must have a key, don't you think?" Penny said.

Judy nodded ruefully. "I should have known someone was keeping an eye on us," she said. "Mum isn't exactly the type not to worry, so with the phone still in and this fellow right around the corner, she might have even arranged for him to look in on us from time to time. This house is old and feels pretty big sometimes so I really don't mind him checking up, I guess."

"I must say I don't mind either," Penny answered. "But where on earth *is* he if his car is still outside?"

A sudden crash made them jump. They looked up the steep staircase and saw a dusty cloud billowing up from a gray paper package that suddenly appeared on the landing. A thump and a thud followed, as yet another two smaller packets landed, shedding bits of shredded paper as they flew through the air. They seemed to come from nowhere and the girls stood gaping, their feet rooted to the cracked linoleum in the front hall. It was only when they craned forward that they noticed the legs of a ladder stretching high up into the upstairs hallway, and disappearing into the trapdoor that covered the way to the attic.

A creaking noise heralded the appearance of two long spindly legs encased in faded blue denim, and a sudden giggle shook Judy as she watched the rest of the old-fashioned overall come into view. The long legs froze in midair, as if stopped short by the spurt of laughter, then continued to descend slowly. Two gnarled hands gripping the sides of the ladder followed and then finally, a leathery face appeared between the rungs.

So this was Bill. A wide smile softened his lined face when he saw the girls, and he lifted a hand in a friendly wave as he lowered himself to the ground. "Hello there. Had a nice day out?"

"Yes, thanks. We did," Judy said politely. "You've been busy here today, haven't you?"

"Oh yes. New window, you know." His head bobbed like a round wooden ball on a spring. "And it's also time to clear out the attic, Mr. Simons said."

"Mr. Simons? Oh, er...yes," Judy awkwardly cleared her throat as she belatedly remembered Uncle Martin's name. "What's this about the attic?"

"Attic conversion, I think he said. Or was it extension?" His eye squinted upward as he carefully lowered the upper half of the ladder alongside the foot on the landing. "Don't know which they'll do, but before they do anything it's got to be cleared out. So that's what I've done today."

"Really? Found anything interesting?"

Penny gave her a playful poke. "Oh sure, Ju. Buried treasure. A priceless antique hidden behind an ancient cobweb. Or what about a lantern to rub? Maybe a genie will appear to help you with your project."

"Very funny." Judy turned to the old man. "Did you? Was there anything up there in the attic?"

"Not much. Mostly papers. Want to see?"

Judy took the steps two at a time while Penny followed

## Chapter Four

behind. The old man poked the bundle on the landing with a leather toe, then coughed a rheumy cough as the dust billowed up again. "I haven't looked through these. They look like record books from some sort of club. Nineteen thirties or thereabouts. Now, that other packet I spent some time over," he admitted, his eyes twinkling as he pointed to the second bundle nearby. "It's old papers — local gossip sheet, more like, and would you believe it, the top one is dated the day I was born."

Penny laughed, then her eyes widened as she took in the date. July 21, 1921.

"Can I help you with that ladder?" she promptly asked, not really wanting to offend him, while realizing he was actually older then he looked.

"No thanks," the old man twinkled. "Shouldn't have told you my birthday, eh?" He winked as he hoisted the ladder with surprising ease and tilted it down the stairwell before him. "You girls bring down the packets instead. They're easier to carry. And I've got something else in here." He patted his pocket. "Not that I think it's worth much. A schoolboy's collection, more like."

"Stamps?"

"No. Coins, I think. Or maybe keys. Something rattling around in a small, metal cigar box."

Bill was right. The old box yielded a heap of dull gray coins and they didn't look like they were of very much value. Though you never can tell, Judy thought hopefully as she poked through the pile where she'd spilled it onto the kichen table. Maybe they'd indeed found a rare treasure worth a fortune for Uncle Martin, and he might even give them a portion of it. She looked up as a throaty chuckle sounded from across the room. Bill was enjoying his gossip sheet.

"Would you believe it? The Old Brass Band! I remember

them playing at the cinema on the corner near the Hill." He laughed at Penny's blank stare. "Oh, way before your time. And they were never really famous, you know. Just for us locals." He flipped through the rest of the pile and grinned. "And it is a music club, isn't it? There's a lot about it in these papers here. I guess that's why they've all been saved."

"Someone here must have been the club treasurer or something," Penny commented, leafing through the record book at the top of the dusty pile. "Dues paid and owed. Very exciting, I must say."

"Oh, it's getting late. And here I am reading this nonsense." Bill set the papers down with a thump. "I'd better be off now. Time for a cuppa tea and my supper."

He went up the sagging kitchen steps to retrieve the ladder he had parked in the front hall. Then he hesitated, shifting awkwardly from one long leg to the other. "Do you think your uncle would let me have that old gossip sheet? Just the one, you know."

"You mean the one with your birthday?" Judy asked, stifling a smile as his head bobbed again on its spring. "I'm sure he wouldn't mind. He probably doesn't even know it still exists. Though I guess you should tell him you took it, next time you speak with him," she added as an afterthought. "You probably will be in touch with him before I will."

The front door shut behind the old man, echoing through the quiet street along with the sound of the ladder thudding onto the min-van. Judy listened for a moment as she heard the old motor cough awake and sputter away around the corner, then she turned back to the kitchen. She yawned as she swept the coins back into the old metal box and shut the lid. "Anything else besides boring old papers and record books?"

## Chapter Four

"Just more of the same," Penny said, pointing to the third packet; yet another mound of newspaper print. "And that's it, Ju. Sorry. No genie. You'll just have to do your work yourself."

Judy ignored the playful remark as she reached for the packet and toyed with the string that was wrapped tightly around it.

"Whose stuff is all this anyway, Ju?" Penny asked as she shuffled the papers back into a pile. "Your Uncle Watsisname?"

"Martin." Judy responded absently as she picked at the stiff knotted string before her, not really intent on undoing it. "My great-great-uncle, I think. My Great-Granny Bess was his sister. But I don't think they ever lived in this house. Granny Bess lived in Ilford and Uncle Martin still lives there. He never married; maybe that's why he feels so close to our family."

"So who did live in this house?" Penny prodded.

Judy looked up and past her, trying to remember. "Maybe Granny Vi, their mother," she said. She paused as the conversation she'd had on the beach slowly came back to her. *My mother had this from hers*, Uncle Martin had said when he'd given her the silver brooch. "Actually, I think it was Granny Vi's mother who lived here." She smiled faintly. "Her name was Yehudis."

A sudden irritation flooded her fingers as she twisted the string on the package again and, as her eyes focused for a better look, her interest quickened: this last packet was different. The sheet of newspaper was not one of a stack, like the others. It was being used as a wrapping for something else inside.

Penny didn't notice Judy's sudden interest. "I'll take this musty heap upstairs," she said, piling the ledgers and record books efficiently together. "Then we can clear this place and have a bite to eat."

Judy mumbled some reply as she scanned the room for something to use as scissors. The vegetable knife was handy and she sawed through the string, the paper shredding to her touch like pencil shavings falling from a sharpener. The paper was older than the others they had found, she realized with growing excitement, and then the string finally snapped, dropping away to the side on the kitchen table.

Still more papers. Judy shuffled through them, her disappointment all the greater after her sudden excitement. Again that inevitable newspaper, only these seemed to be bits and pieces clipped and neatly folded, rather than complete editions stacked in a pile. And envelopes. About ten of them, with their stamps cut off. No chance of a treasure there, Judy thought ruefully, as she carefully reached into one and withdrew a thin white sheet of paper. It was covered with bold black writing, as if written with a blunt nib dipped in heavy India ink, and the script was round and clear. But not clear enough for her to decipher it, Judy realized, and she remembered the loops and whirls on her silver brooch. The page was covered with Hebrew script.

So were the newspaper clippings, Judy was astonished to find as she quickly thumbed through a few of them. Did people really print Hebrew newspapers? She wondered who actually read them, and who had gathered these cuttings into a neat pile and sorted them away in the attic.

She started suddenly as a creak sounded on the stairs.

"Anything else to get rid of, Judy?" Penny called down over the railing. "I've piled the stuff in that other bedroom. We can't really throw anything out without your uncle's say-so, can we?"

## Chapter Four

"No. Just leave it all there," Judy absently called back. She found herself hurriedly stuffing her find back into a haphazard pile, retying the string any which way. For some reason, she didn't want Penny to see it. Maybe she'd get a chance to go through it more carefully sometime; there might be something in English that she could decipher. She wondered if the girl next door could read the Hebrew script. Somehow, she didn't want to wait to ask Uncle Martin about it when he next visited down at the sea.

As Penny thudded cheerfully down the steps, Judy stood up suddenly and slung her jacket over her arm, concealing the little bundle under it. She stepped carefully past Penny as they passed each other in the doorway. "Just going to wash up a bit," she said casually. "Won't be a minute."

Once upstairs, she thrust the papers deep into the inside pocket of her rucksack and zipped it up. For some strange reason, she felt that they belonged there right now; stored away with her private belongings.

They didn't have cheese toast for supper that night. Instead they heated up some tinned soup and made salmon sandwiches. But when they got into bed, it was still the same old story. Penny's sleeping bag was exactly that: a bag that sent her off to sleep at the very moment she got into it, while Judy lay as stiff as the floorboards that were creaking throughout the house, and sleep just would not come. Tonight again, she could hear the indistinct murmur from the house next door. Jewish studies, she thought to herself, and grimaced. How boring. Enough to put anyone to sleep. She wondered how many people were snoring through the speech on the other side of the fireplace while she lay here, a frustrated insomniac.

After what seemed like endless hours, Judy could

hear the scraping and thumping that signaled the end of the lecture. The voices sounded surprisingly alert and cheerful; maybe they were just happy it was over, a nasty little voice inside her said. So what made them come in the first place? another little voice challenged.

*Impatient with all these little voices, Judy decided to go downstairs to assume her position at the board. She had reached the doorway of the dark bedroom before she remembered that the board with the convenient crack was no longer there. She hesitated a moment, staring down the steep staircase by the light of the single bulb on the hallway landing. Putting a tentative foot forward, she wondered if she should return to her bed, when a sudden rustle beneath her made her realize that she was really still in bed, zipped inside her sleeping bag. Half of her consciousness could feel the warmth of her blanket, wrapped around her as she lay flat on the floor, and the other half stood on the very top stair. The front room door stood open and Judy suddenly realized that a warm light was streaming out from it, brighter than any streetlight could be, filtered through a new white blind. A familiar warmth seemed to spread itself out into the hall together with the light, drifting up the stairs to where Judy stood, and wrapping itself around her like a fluffy, cozy blanket.*

*"I'm dreaming," she thought to herself. "This isn't really happening."*

*But she let herself go. Her back arched as she was brought slowly down the steps and gently deposited at the front room door which stood open, as if to welcome her in.*

CHAPTER FIVE

The fire crackled a warm greeting as its light merged with the deep yellow shine of the table lamp, and filled the room with a quiet glow. Judy recognized the array of ornaments on the mantlepiece below the stately mirror, only this time she did not have to strain to see reflections in the glass. She could feel the soft nap of the flowered carpet warming her toes as she stepped just over the threshold, her eyes taking in the heavy lace curtains hanging where the white blinds had been, the massive paintings on the walls, the wax fruit under a glass case on the small table in the corner. The room seemed so crowded with furniture; armchairs and sofas all clustered around the polished dark table that stood in the center, and she didn't know where to look first. Then a sudden movement to her right caught her eye and with a start, Judy realized that she was not alone.

A small slight figure in a white ruffled blouse was sitting on the deep plush overstuffed armchair at the side of the fire. Judy could see the glint of the knitting needles in her hands as they flashed expertly in and out of the dusty rose-colored shawl that was spread out over her long, full, navy blue skirt. She looked up for a moment and Judy shrank back against the half-open door, but the woman wasn't looking her way. Judy followed her gaze across to the opposite wall where a roll-top desk stood along a mahogany book case with glass-paned doors. A broad-shouldered man with a full black beard was seated in the high-backed arm chair, his head bent over the large open book before him.

Judy felt as if she were intruding on this homey scene; she should back out of the room, but the warmth of the fire was enticing, enjoining her to say. Her feet, on their own accord, took a step forward instead, but she suddenly found that she could go no further. It was as if an invisible barrier stood in her way, and she remembered the hazy curtain that she had strained to see through the last time she stood at this door. Now the view was clear; she could see every last bobble on the crocheted cloth that covered the mahogany table. Through the invisible glass, she could even hear the quiet settling of the coals in the grate. But the barrier was firmly in place and allowed her no entry; she would just have to be content to stay where she was and look and listen.

For a moment, Judy felt as if she were observing the waxen figures at Madame Tussaud's. Then the nimble fingers that seemed to move by some power of their own, suddenly were still and the woman in the armchair looked up at the door where Judy was standing.

Judy tried to turn and run, but it was as if her feet were rooted in cement and she could not move from her place. She felt herself go pink with discomfort and her lips worked soundlessly as she cast about for some lame explanation: what was she doing standing and staring in at their door? Then a sudden current of air swished by her and she realized that the woman did not even see her. Instead, her gaze was fixed on the spot just at Judy's right where a young girl of about twleve or thirteen had

## Chapter Five

*just entered the room. Judy could feel the thick gray fabric of the girl's heavy smocked dress brush past her as she slipped through the doorway, past the barrier where Judy could not go.*

*"There you are, Chaya'le." A bright smile softened the careworn face of the woman on the armchair as she patted the plush footstool before her invitingly. "Finished all that work the teacher gave you? Why don't you come and join us?"*

*For a moment the child hesitated, then she said hastily, "I'm just going out for a little while, Mama. You don't mind, do you?" she said persuasively. "Jennifer has a new Captain Marryat book that she promised I could borrow. I'll be back soon, don't worry."*

*A shadow crossed her mother's gentle face. "Take your coat, Chaya'le. It's cold outside."*

*"Oh, don't worry so much, Mama," she pouted. "It's just three houses down the next street." She tossed her bright curls over her shoulder and was gone, with a slam of the front door that sounded through the quiet room like a slap in the face.*

*The only movement in the room was the quiet swish of the heavy lace curtains, swaying in the breeze brought in by the opening and shutting of the door. The woman sat still in her chair, her knitting forgotten, her face a quiet mask of hidden feelings as she gazed into the fire. Judy turned her attention to the man at the desk; something about the set of his shoulders and the arch of his back told her that while his eyes may have been fixed on the page before him, his mind was elsewhere. A gentle sigh from his wife brought his head up abruptly.*

*"You didn't have to let her go." His words were a strange blend of plea and accusation.*

*"No?" That single syllable, uttered in such an expres-*

sionless tone, spoke volumes. For a moment, he turned back to his book, then abandoned all attempts at further concentration. He turned his gaze back to the woman in the chair, still staring unhappily into the fire. His eyebrows drew together in irritation.

"Still thinking of the old place in the East End? Pining for your dungeon below Moses Levy's Boots and Shoes?"

"Don't be silly." His wife looked up at him in gentle reproof. She looked around the ornate room, but her eyes seemed to stare vacantly right past the furniture. Then she smiled. "Don't look like a thundercloud, Leibel," she said softly. "You do your best, I know. But I worry."

"You always worry," he answered, his black beard bristling as his chin came out belligerently. "But what on earth you worry about, I really don't know. You no longer have to worry about the slimy steps down to our cellar flat, the damp walls and windows that leaked with every rainstorm. Or even about the pleurisy that Kalman next door developed because of it all, and you were so frightened it would happen to us."

"Chas v'shalom!" the woman shivered.

"Or would you rather worry that Chaya'le needs a new pair of shoes?" he went on relentlessly. "And we were too hungry to go without dinner for a while in order to have money to buy them. Are you forgetting?" His voice rose. "Are you forgetting that terrible time before we met Itche, and we went to Bethnal Green market to see if the silk factories would hire Chaya'le for the day? Do you remember the nine-year-old girls that stood there, wringing their red chapped hands into their balled up petticoats to try and warm them, begging the men to choose them for work? You took one look at that dreadful scene, the shouting, the coarse people who stood there, and you grabbed Chaya'le by the hand and ran for your

## Chapter Five

life." He laughed grimly. "You were a block away before I could catch you," he said. "And the very next day, we met Itche."

He looked around the room with quiet satisfaction and then turned back to her. "Look at us now. An entire house to yourself with every convenience I could buy you. No more dragging home heavy buckets of water from the standpipe at the street corner. No more fish barrows leaking down your windowsill." His voice softened. "Look at you now," he said. "Sitting like a lady by the fire, knitting yourself a shawl, instead of sewing your eyes out for Mottel the tailor."

He smiled gently. "Why don't you look outside," he added. "The trees, the green hedges, the garden in the back. Breathe in the healthy air. It's a long way from Hounsditch." He fingered the soft green fringe of the mat on his desk. "Look at all this. And you worry? What are you worrying about?"

His wife looked around the room for a moment, and then she sighed. "These things are all lovely, Leibel. You've done so well and you look so important going off in your bowler to the Underground train each morning. And best of all, you've won your weekly Shabbos battle. Itche even lets you leave early on the short Friday afternoons. He would never make you come in on Shabbos and Yom Tov, even though he himself makes kiddush and opens the warehouse afterwards. But the people..."

Her voice trailed off and they both looked again towards the doorway, where moments ago, Chaya'le had stood before she flitted off to Jennifer.

Jennifer. The name seemed to shout in the stillness even though neither had vocalized it.

"Can't she make friends in shul?"

"Shul?" she smiled sadly at his anxious face. "Very few

*girls come to shul. We try to go every Shabbos. It's not that far to Lordship Park and Chaya'le tries to be good about it. But very few women come with children. It's far for them to walk and boring for them once they're there. You know what a battle it is each week."* Her voice broke as she let out the words. *"Last weekend, Chaya'le wanted to stay at Jennifer's. I didn't tell you about it, but you did see her sulking all Shabbos morning, didn't you? That's because I didn't let her go."*

This time, Leibel stared silently into the fire, as if trying to find a solution there for all his problems. *"I don't really understand,"* he finally said impatiently. *"Who was there for her to play with when we lived in the East End? Ruchke's daughters who slept under the barrow each night because there was no room for them down in the cellar?"*

She turned on him suddenly. *"Really, Leibel! I prefer Ruchke's daughters, dirty as they were, to high-and-mighty Jennifer. Don't you see why I worry? Are you blind?"* She picked up a knitting needle and looked at it reflectively. *"I would be happier to see Chaya'le running out near Petticoat Lane to play 'Warning,' than sitting elegantly in Jennifer's parlor, discussing her latest book."*

*" 'Warning?' "*

She smiled for a moment, remembering, and then she chanted softly.

*"Warning once, warning twice, warning three times over!*

*A bushel of wheat and a bushel of rye,*

*When cock crows, out jump I,*

*Warning! Warning! Wa-rr-nin-ing!"*

Judy watched with fascination as small black shadows began to dance across the white lace curtains at the window, like figures in a film on a brightly lit screen. She

## Chapter Five

*could see one grimy little girl separate herself from the crowd and, clasping her hands together, she called out the Warning as the other children scattered. Hands still clasped above her faded pinafore, the little girl rushed out towards the ragged figures that danced away before her, her thin cotton dress swirling about her in a crooked line. She gasped and giggled as she ran after the flitting children, reaching out to touch one somehow, with an elbow or a toe, trying all the while to keep her balance as her hands still gripped together tightly. One small figure fell down in the mud and she jabbed her with her knee.*

"Got you!" *she exclaimed.*

*Now two little girls joined hands and chased the ragged figures down the cobblestone road. Judy watched them scamper about, their long thin braids streaming out behind them, as they chased the crowd of children. One by one, other children were caught and joined to the chain, until a long line of hunters was chasing and hemming in the other players. Only the girls at each end had free hands to catch them as they ran. Finally, with one swift grab, the last laughing girl was captured and the game ended. The squealing and shouting gradually died out, as if a volume knob was being turned down slowly but surely, and the string of ragged dancing children disappeared into the distance. Only thin lace patterns could now be seen on the long white curtains at the window.*

"Warning." The woman whispered the word gently in the now quiet room and she turned to her husband sadly. "Don't you see? It was a chain of children, all the same kind, and they kept out the strangers. Here she has no protection. The neighborhood school has only Jennifers and Janes. No Ruchkes or Mirels. And now Chaya'le is Vivian. Vivian!"

"'Can Vi come out to play?'" she mimicked. "A school

*we need, not a shul," she said sadly.*

*"A school." Her husband laughed shortly. "Who should I start a school with? With Mendel who calls himself Martin and says he's had enough of running away from Cossacks? With Chunia who says his wife Sophie wants their Yankel to be a doctor? A doctor!" he snorted. "He'll be busy trying to make everyone well while his own neshamah will be sick."*

*He turned to her softly. "But what can we do, Yehudis? We can only try to do our best."*

*Judy stood stock-still in the doorway. Yehudis. Was this the Yehudis of the brooch? she wondered, and all at once she knew that it was. She closed her eyes for a moment and when she opened them, she saw that the scene behind the glass barrier was fading fast. The dark mahogany furniture, the wax and china ornaments, the paintings and the mirror, were all blending rapidly into the stripes on the wallpaper, until only the tall brass candlesticks remained on the mantlepiece, hazily reflecting the anxious faces of the husband and wife. Then they faded away as well, leaving Judy standing alone in the empty front room, staring soundlessly at the peeling blue paint above the boarded up fireplace. But only for a moment, for the front room finally faded into the darkness, as Judy slept.*

It was an uneasy sleep, in which Judy kept feeling around beneath her, as if to reassure herself that she was still safe inside her sleeping bag and not floating off downstairs. Every few moments she woke with a start, staving off the deeper slumber that could bring with it dreams, then glanced around the bare room with a strange sense of relief. Only towards morning did she finally sink into a quiet sleep, her body relaxing into the cushioning vinyl beneath her.

## Chapter Five

It was the urgent sound of a honking van that finally woke her, its insistent horn prodding her awake as the sounds of the street filtered through the haze of her mind. Judy stretched and yawned, grateful for that extra breath of air before she opened her eyes. She could hear voices calling as the street pulsed with life and, easing her way out of the sleeping bag, she padded over to the window.

Judy watched with fascination as doors opened and shut; mothers and children emerged from every end of the street as several vans stood ready for departure. For a moment Judy wondered if she had tumbled into yet another dream, with more strange sights and costumes to see and absorb. Tiny boys climbed into a yellow van, their long sidelocks flying as they waved to their mothers who clutched their kerchiefs in the December bluster.

"Leibel! Your lunch! Again you've forgotten it!" shouted one stout woman as she raced out of her house, a small string of toddlers following behind her, waddling along like ducklings behind their mother.

Vying for space in the narrow road, a dark blue van waited impatiently as two girls, obviously sisters, identically dressed in dark decorum, made their way leisurely out of their house, ignoring the tiny tot who shouted from the window:

"Bye, Chaya! Bye, Mirel! Have a nice day!"

The names reverberated in the air as the scene of last night's dream replayed in her mind, like the film that had danced on the white lace curtains of the Victorian parlor. Judy stared at the faces and figures below her and wondered. Had she dreamed it all in the few short morning moments as the strange names sounded through the streets? Somehow, she hardly thought so. The gleam of the brass candlesticks shone in her memory, their reflection softened in the pink tinged mirror, like a scene in some historical documentary that must lurk somewhere in the recesses of her mind. From where could her subconscious have conjured up that whole scene? The names, the details, the strange, foreign words that peppered the conversations...yet something deeper brushed at the edge of her awareness — something very unusual. What was it?

Judy struggled with her memory of the dream until she finally hit on it: she sensed that she had not merely dreamed about these characters, but actually had merged with them, somehow. She had *felt their feelings.* She shuddered involuntarily. How very odd. She vaguely remembered a biology lesson on hidden memories coming to the fore and felt a bit better, her feet finding a more solid footing on the floorboards as she gazed into the street. The last door had shut and the vans were well on their way. The only movements below her were the bare tree branches swaying in the wind.

## Chapter Six

Judy came down to the kitchen to find Penny poring over a large London Transport map that was spread over the breakfast table like some garishly patterned tablecloth.

"Good morning, Sleepyhead," Penny greeted her amiably between noisy crunches of bran flakes. She picked up her coffee mug and eyed Judy through the wisps of steam that curled up lazily towards the ceiling. "For someone who's slept till almost ten o'clock, you look awfully woozy."

Penny liked her coffee hot and strong; Judy could almost taste it as its pungent smell knifed through the fog in her brain. It felt good.

"Looks like you're just having breakfast," she grinned. "You must not be up very long."

"Not too long," Penny admitted. "But you're the one with so much to do. I thought you'd be sitting there with your nose to the grindstone for hours already."

"I'm still at the fact-finding stage," Judy said defensively. She looked at the stack of colorful brochures beside Penny's cereal bowl. "You have quite an agenda this morning, I see. Where are you off to today?"

Penny's mouth curved upwards in a barely concealed smile of amusement. "Where am *I* off to? Are you planning to stay home and work?" she asked with exaggerated surprise. Then her basic good nature took over. "Sorry, Ju. Didn't mean to boss you around," she apologized. "Are you in the mood for playing tourist again, or would you rather stay home and get some work done while I go out?"

Judy hesitated. How could she explain that she was in no frame of mind for a lighthearted day out about town? But the thought of staying behind alone in the house did not exactly tempt her. Not that I'm afraid, Judy hastened to assure herself. Last night was, after all, only a dream, and not even a nightmare at that. But still, it was so very real that every time she passed by the front room, she half expected to see it fill up with furniture. With Penny away, she was sure that every sound or squeak that might disturb the stillness of the empty house would bring her up and out of her seat, wondering what she was going to see next. It's like getting a crank call in the middle of the night, a call that jerks you up in the middle of a deep sleep. You hang up fast and tell yourself it's nothing. But all the rest of the night you lie there tensed up, waiting for that phone to ring again.

Judy turned away to the kitchen counter and poured herself a bowl of cereal with slow and deliberate motions. "What are you planning?" she asked casually, as she took a seat at the breakfast table and looked over Penny's shoulder at the *Visitor's Guide to London*.

Penny pointed down at the expanse of blue which marked the River Thames. "How about the Tower of London?" she suggested. "It's such a beautiful day. Just the right weather for wandering around there. There's supposed to be tons to see." Her finger mapped a route up from the square marked Tower Hill. "If we still have any energy left when we've finished, we could walk up to Petticoat Lane Market. I think it's open on Fridays.

Chapter Six

Maybe I could get something cheap for my Mum as a coming home present."

Penny traced a line down the main road, ending up at the crossroad of Stamford Hill. "You know, we're not really all that far from the Tower of London," she said. "Look, the 253 bus would take us almost straight there. But the traffic!"

She rummaged in the pile of pamphlets for the Underground guide. "It's probably a case of the longer route being the fastest," she said. "I think I'll stick to the train." She looked up at Judy. "Well, are you coming along?"

Petticoat Lane. At the sound of the words, Judy's fingers had frozen onto her spoon. Her eyes were riveted on the line Penny's finger had just traced on the glossy map. Halfway down the paper the words *Bethnal Green* leaped out at her; her insides gave a lurch that had nothing to do with the soggy bran flakes she'd just swallowed. There was no way she was going to stay alone in this house today, even if it meant trailing behind Penny and rummaging through stalls of bric-a-brac for some white elephant to bring home to Mum.

The sun was unusually bright for a December day as Judy and Penny settled themselves on a bench to the side of the square. Carefully avoiding the sight of the stone where Ann Boleyn had lost her head, they busied themselves unwrapping sandwiches and opening drink cartons. Penny sighed as she stretched her aching legs out before her. "We really should have left the jewels for last," she commented, taking a sip of her juice. "There's nothing much worth seeing after that, is there?"

Judy absently agreed. The crown jewels really were something, she had to admit; it was unbelievable to think that the ornate crowns and scepters, the jeweled scabbards and solid gold tableware — all had once been in ordinary use by the reigning monarch. But in the darkness of the jewel vault, she had suddenly gone dizzy. The lights in the dim underground room were focused only on the glass cases where the dazzling treasures were displayed on purple velvet, and for a moment she had felt as if she were once again looking through a clear barrier at a lit up scene. Then Penny had gripped her arm with excitement, bringing her thankfully back to reality, if a solid gold, castle-shaped salt cellar that took up half a table could be called reality.

"Will you look at that?" Penny had laughed. "Now just imagine the scene at the royal table if somebody filled it with pepper!"

The two girls had been seized with a fit of giggles that was only made worse by the stares they were getting from the people around them. Everyone seemed to be tiptoing past the glass showcases, speaking in hushed, reverent tones while they were laughing hysterically as if they were standing before the monkey cage in the zoo. It was only when the sudden glare of sunlight hit them as they came up from the subterranean reaches under the White Tower that they sobered up.

"Actually," Judy commented as she took a bite of her sandwich. "Now you know what they mean in the books when they talk about someone seated above or below the salt. You know, the higher rank fellows sat at the table ahead of it and the lower downs sat below."

"Well, that thing is humongous! Who were the ones who sat alongside it?"

"The ones with high blood pressure."

Penny groaned. She balled up her sandwich wrapping and threw it playfully at Judy. "Time to move on," she said briskly, gathering up their bits and pieces and squashing

## Chapter Six

it all into a nearby overflowing rubbish bin. "There are a few more buildings that we haven't been into."

Half an hour later, they agreed again that they should have left the jewels for last. They eyed with faint distaste the numerous exhibits of assorted weapons and torture equipment that had been improved and remodeled over the centuries, then moved on to the displays of armor, but they were beginning to feel they'd had enough. One last tower looked tempting, with an original spiral stone staircase to climb to get to the top. The stones beneath their feet and on the walls on either side were cold and slimy with a thickness measured in feet, not inches. Judy could picture the prisoners slowly climbing up to their cells, heavy chains clanking as they hauled themselves up the steep stairs. She felt along the side wall to her left for support; there was no railing on the other side and when she looked down she could see the people behind them craning their necks upwards to see how much higher they had to go. It was like climbing up and around the sides of a wall. She wondered how they were going to get down; it was only up and up. The down staircase must be over on the other side.

They finally reached the top and it was like coming out of a time warp back into the twentieth century. Through the stainless steel gateway at the top they could see yet another display of armor and weapons in a large hall, well-lit by fluorescent fixtures, but the gate was locked. In order to enter the exhibit hall, the way led through the dim crypt of an ancient chapel, as old as the staircase they'd just climbed. Penny led the way and Judy found herself hesitating before the ornate archway, with a strange reluctance to enter. She pictured herself trying to climb back down that winding one-way staircase and she knew that was impossible. For a moment, she was almost tempted to ask the guards if they would open the gateway for her; they looked friendly and she was sure they wouldn't mind. But somehow, with her eyes closed, she managed to follow mechanically behind Penny. When she opened her eyes, she found herself in the exhibit hall, her face averted from the alien room at the left. She looked down and realized she was gripping her necklace chain tightly, as if holding onto some lifeline that would carry her through.

Judy smiled; the irony of the small gold chain that dangled empty over her pullover did not escape her. Initials had been all the rage last summer. Every girl in the class had a big block letter hanging from a chain; solid silver or gold, depending on her father's pocket. Penny still had her *P*, but Judy's chain was empty. She had removed her *J* after their autumn history course that had detailed the rise and fall of Nazi Germany. It was not quite a yellow star or a *J* stamped into her passport, yet if it would have been a *B* or a *P*, she wouldn't have taken it off. Now here she was, clutching the place where her *J* had been, realizing how nice it would be to have it now, giving her a bit of a secure feeling from home. And now she remembered the graceful swirls of the Hebrew lettering on the silver brooch, and she was glad Uncle Martin had given it to her, even if it was back at home, safe in her mother's jewelry box.

Penny had gone through the archway quickly. "Funny thing, that," she said suddenly, nodding her head towards the dark crypt they'd just left. "For people who were always knocking everyone's heads off, they were awfully religious. There must be at least half a dozen chapels in this place."

Judy stared at Penny with a bemused expression on her face. "What do you mean — *they?*" she said. "For all

## Chapter Six

you know it was your grandfather who sat in that pew."

Penny stared. "My grandfather?" she gaped. "What on earth do you mean? My grandfather was a fisherman a few miles down the coast from our place!"

Judy smiled. Penny was a wonderfully loyal friend but she could be awfully thick at times. "I don't mean your grandfather, silly," she said gently. "Maybe great-great. Or make that great-great to the tenth power."

Penny wrinkled her nose. "Really, Judy," she laughed. "I have enough trouble keeping track of my grandparents and Great-Aunt Doris. If anyone ever came to this glorified dungeon a hundred years ago, they weren't relatives of mine."

Judy left it at that. But this short conversation would come back to her just a little while later.

The girls descended the spacious staircase at the other side of the tower and headed straight for the exit gate. Judy looked at her watch; for some reason, she felt the urge to be home by nightfall. "When do you want to get home?" she asked.

"It's quite early still, isn't it? But it's getting a bit colder," Penny answered, zipping up her anorak. "The sun has gone in. I hope it won't rain." She looked up at the darkening sky. "I don't want to be back late, though. Let's get home before dark."

They crossed the gateway that had once been a chain drawbridge spanning a deep moat. A lush green lawn now sloped down from the turreted walls of the castle, covering the banks where water had lapped at the stone. From there, it was a brisk walk through twentieth-century traffic; carefully signposted curves skimmed their speeding vehicles along past gleaming office buildings. Then they entered a cluster of roads that led in and out of each other, Judy panting along beside Penny as she strode ahead confidently.

"You memorize the map or something?" Judy asked, as they came to yet another one-way road lined with blank faced brick houses that looked like they were frozen to the pavement.

Penny laughed. "More or less," she answered. "Actually, just the names of the streets we need to follow." She looked up to where two street signs hung side by side, marking the corner where two roads met midway. "Here's where *Crutched Friars* meets *Jewry Street*. Then we've just got two main roads to cross."

Judy looked up at the street signs and stopped in her tracks. "Jewry Street! Why do they call it that?"

Penny shrugged her shoulders as she continued on her way, not noticing the expression on Judy's face. "Don't really know. I think this area dates back a long way, though. One of the brochures said this place was a ghetto of sorts back in Medieval times. Don't think you'll find any Jews here now." She wrinkled her nose at the dull facades. "Doesn't look like you'll find *anyone* living here, for that matter."

Judy was silent for the next stretch of their walk. Why should she be moved at the thought of the people who had walked these streets centuries ago? she wondered. She thought of Penny and her Aunt Doris and she grinned wryly to herself. The *J* that she had removed from her chain was haunting her. There had been ghettoes here in London too, she mused. Then an expulsion, she remembered vaguely. But the Jews had come back. The two girls crossed Aldgate and then Judy saw the next street sign. *Hounsditch*. The Jews *had* come back, it seemed, to the very same area they had lived in centuries before.

The final few roads flew past Judy in a strange sort

## Chapter Six

of haze. Penny was chattering happily about what sort of thing she thought her mother might like, but Judy did not hear a word. So this was the East End. She could see where lanes and alleys wound past warehouses and factories, and she wondered if this was where Leibel had come each morning on the train. Or was his warehouse located in some other area, and those Exchange Buildings she could see were standing on a street that had been cleared of its slums. Smaller shopfronts lined the side street they were passing as they neared the market and she wondered: had Moses Levy once sold his boots and shoes in one of those shops near the corner and was that metal pavement square just below the dusty display window, the opening to Ruchke's basement room? Those ragged, shadowy figures that had danced across the white lace curtains last night were etched on Judy's brain. She could picture those children racing down the road towards the market, scampering among the stalls and barrows piled up with goods and merchandise of every description.

The two girls entered the market area and began to browse among the colorful displays. Anything and everything was offered for sale, from bicycles to bananas and lots of things in between. The attractively arranged stalls were a magnet for bargain-hunting tourists, but Judy imagined the stalls as they must have looked to the children playing *Warning* to warm their frozen, rag-wrapped feet. Piles of shabby second-hand clothing, mounds of potatoes sprouting eyes, fish barrows leaking onto the uneven pavement beneath them, perhaps a stall of trinkets to liven up the dismal scene. But the chant of the children echoed in her mind and she remembered the cheerful sound of their voices, the eager clasp of their hands as they danced down the street.

Judy's fingers tugged again at the chain around her neck. It still had not broken under pressure; the jeweler had assured her it was good quality and strong. For some reason, the words of Yehudis came back to her: *a chain of children that kept out the strangers.* She looked at Penny walking along happily beside her, oblivious to the turmoil in Judy's mind, and she realized just how far her family had traveled from Hounsditch. That chain of children had broken and the family had wandered even further afield from Kyverdale Road. Great-Granny Bess had lived in Ilford; Judy remembered visiting her. Its spacious houses were more suited to her suburban lifestyle. So did her daughter, Judy's grandmother. And now Judy and her parents lived in a modern cottage by the sea. Judy remembered how she had sat with Uncle Martin, watching the relentless return of the sea to its twelve-hour mark of the tide, and her fingers once again absently twisted the thin golden chain that hung at her neck.

The steady whine of a vacuum cleaner greeted the two girls as they staggered wearily into the house. For a moment, they thought it was their house being cleaned, but then the Hoover stopped and the by now familiar series of bumps and thumps sounded from next door. There was no scraping of chairs and tables, however, and then the back door was flung open and they could hear the splash of water flowing down the garden drain.

"Just an ordinary weekend cleanup," Penny commented, as she unwrapped their market purchases. She held up a small china vase and gazed at it with obvious satisfaction. "Mum loves to put out single roses cut from our prize garden bush," she said. "This vase is just the right size." She turned to Judy. "You bought the bigger one, didn't you?"

## Chapter Six

Judy shrugged. "I didn't put much thought into it," she admitted. "Mum likes a big bunch of flowers at a time and besides, it's a nice shade of pink. I think she'll be happy."

She turned her head towards the wall that divided them from the house next door. "It seems to have quieted down over there," she said thoughtfully. A hushed sense of calm seemed to blanket the house next door, seeping out into the street and somehow into the room where they sat. Judy wondered if Penny could feel it too. Penny was sprawled out at the kitchen table, immersed in a detective novel, but Judy could not bring herself to do a thing. For a moment she wondered if it was a good time to look through the papers she'd hidden in her backpack, but a strange reluctance still filled her at the thought of sharing them with Penny. Instead, she hauled out her geography book and tried to settle down to work. She found the guidelines for her coursework, but the small close print danced on the page and her eyes focused instead on the white spaces between the letters and words. With a sigh, she finally gave up and looked up to find Penny eyeing her, a bit of a mother hen in her quiet smile.

"Why don't you forget it and come to bed early, Judy," she said. "We did do a lot of walking today, didn't we?"

Judy had to agree and she shut her book in relief. It felt good to crawl into her sleeping bag and a peaceful drowsiness overcame her as she lay listening to the small still sounds that traveled up the chimney. The family next door seemed still to be seated around their dining room table. She could hear snatches of cheerful singing from behind the plaster, occasionally the clink of a plate. She stretched and turned over for a better position, but the sound of the papers rustling beneath her blocked her final fall into sleep.

Stealing a glance at the second sleeping bag, Judy could see that Penny was fast asleep. Moving quietly so as not to wake her, she gingerly withdrew the packet from its hiding place. Tiptoeing into the hallway, she settled herself on the very top step, where the lightbulb welcomed her with a quiet glow. For a moment, Judy wondered if she would find herself floating down the stairs, feet first, and she patted the pockmarked linoleum on the step to make sure that she really was there. She smiled as the cold on her palm reassured her. This time, at least, she was certain that she was fully awake.

The newspaper shredded into her lap as she untied the single knot she'd hurriedly tied the day before. Putting the newspaper aside, Judy turned her attention first to the envelopes. She stacked them in a tidy heap, but couldn't find any particular order. When were postmarks invented? she wondered. In any case, whatever identifying dates there might have been would have been cut away with the stamps. Not all the handwritings were the same, she discovered, even though each letter was addressed to the house on Kyverdale Road, but every envelope was addressed in an awkward script, as if laboriously copied from a sheet that the writer couldn't read. *L. Schumacher.* She read the name slowly to herself, savoring each syllable. It was totally unfamiliar, except, perhaps, for the first initial. *L.* She wondered.

Judy slipped out one page after the other, always careful to reinsert each letter into its correct envelope, but she couldn't find anything that she could understand. Sometimes the handwriting was bold and cursive and sometimes graceful and small, but always it was in a definite Hebrew script that refused to admit her into its secrets. At one point Judy thought she had made a breakthrough: one envelope had a return address that

## Chapter Six

at first glance seemed to be ordinary English lettering. But it proved to be indecipherable. Russian? Any guess would do; Judy had to admit defeat.

The newspapers too were frustrating. No swirls and whirls on the printed page, but the square squat letters seemed to turn their inscrutable gaze on Judy, as she carefully unfolded and refolded each one in its turn, failing to break their code. Only one page had a masthead and it was actually in English print: *The Express*, May 5, 1903. Judy blinked and looked at the date again, the grip of her finger softening as she suddenly realized how very old the packet was. Then, at the next clipping in the pile, she stopped. Photographs.

There were several pictures and Judy held each of them up to the light, but they were gray and grainy, and it was hard to make out exactly what they were meant to be. Odd that someone should take snapshots of rubbish heaps and print them on the front page of a newspaper. One of the photographs seemed to show bolts of shredded material thrown in a haphazard heap, while the second depicted all sorts of broken furniture, piled outside a corner house. Judy could make no sense of it all, and she was growing tired of unfolding and refolding unreadable papers.

"Judy?"

The sudden call from the bedroom made her jump and she thrust the papers beneath her with one swift motion. "Penny? It's okay. I'm here. Coming right in."

Judy carefully put the papers together, trying not to rustle them loudly enough for Penny to hear. Holding the packet inconspicuously under her arm, she climbed back into her sleeping bag, waiting for Penny to fall asleep before slipping the papers back into their hiding place. She lay there, willing sleep to come, yet hoping that the strange double act would follow, with half of her warm in her sleeping bag and half of her descending the stairs. When the familiar floating sensation began to prick at her back and the dream began, she welcomed it. She wanted to go downstairs again, to see what she could see in the front room tonight.

CHAPTER SEVEN

The room was just as Judy remembered it, only this time it seemed brighter and, for a moment, she couldn't decide why. The massive paintings, done in shades of deepest reds and browns, were still there, as were the graceful tinted mirror, the richly striped wallpaper, and the dark mahogany furniture hugging the walls. But it was the color white that leaped out and held her eye: a starched white tablecloth covered the oval table that dominated the center of the room and, where a bowl of wax fruit in a glass case had been, two white candles flickered from their perch in a graceful pair of brass candlesticks, polished to a high shine.

Judy could see that the candles must have been especially tall to start with; a wedge of melted wax gathered around the stems as if reluctant to leave the scene. By now, only two slender stubs remained but the flames were still steady and, reflected in the stately mirror, they appeared brighter than the fire that was already burning low in the grate.

As Judy stepped closer to the invisible barrier that still seemed to be in place, she could suddenly sense the warm smell of cooking that hung about the room. Scattered crumbs on the patterned carpet and a few telltale spots on *the white cloth told her that the man and woman seated at the table had just finished their meal and she wished she could have joined them sooner. She wondered if they had also sung cheerful songs like those she had heard from the house next door. The room was awash with the same sense of peace that had seeped through the brickwork this evening, after the whining and splashing sounds of cleaning had stopped. That sense of peace seemed to radiate out of the glowing lights of the candles.*

*This time, the man was seated at the table, instead of the desk, but the same large book was spread open before him. His dark hair fell forward as he bent over it, oblivious to the sweet-faced woman seated opposite him in the brocade upholstered chair. Her dark blue dress was made of shiny stiff material, and a row of jet black buttons marched down the front, as if advancing towards the starched white cloth before her. Perched just under the little ruffled collar was an oblong silver bar pin, etched with delicate swirls.* Yehudis.

*She was holding a small thick book in her hand, a slender forefinger daintily pointing to the bold black letters on the page, and Judy tried to see if she could recognize any writing. The woman looked up then, and Judy held her breath, in a strange way wanting to be noticed, but the dark eyes only clouded as Yehudis looked right past her, through the doorway into the empty hall, and she sighed as she turned back to her little book.*

*Her husband looked up at the sound. "It's getting late," he observed, eyeing the black and gold clock on the mantlepiece. "Chaya'le's not back yet?"*

*"No."*

*"Should I go fetch her home?"*

*"No." Her voice went up an octave and the single syllable was charged with a current that flowed as surely as*

## Chapter Seven

*the heat from the fire in the grate.*

"Yehudis!" His voice rose in tandem with his thick black brows. "Are you becoming afraid of that child?"

"Leibel, please," she said tensely, her face turning white as she spoke. "Afraid?" She swallowed, then tried to soften her tone. "Leibel, don't you see? There are so many things that come up between us each day. Sixty minutes an hour, twenty-four hours a day. I must decide — do I make an issue of some particular thing, or do I just pretend I don't see or hear?"

"What do you mean, pretend? If she's doing something she shouldn't, of course you make an issue!"

Yehudis sighed. "It's not so simple, Leibel," she said gently. "Look at tonight. She knows she must help for Shabbos, must be here when Shabbos comes in. She mustn't go with her friends on the tramway to Clapton Pond on Shabbos. And she knows because I've firmly said NO so many times. But I can't always say no. I must decide when yes and when no, and that's what makes me afraid."

The fire crackled quietly as he tried to absorb her words.

"Look," Yehudis continued. "Chaya'le was good all day. She peeled potatoes and brought the coals up from the basement. In Jennifer's house on Portland Avenue, only Martha does such work."

"Martha?"

"The maid. You see? And Chaya'le did it all nicely and happily. She loves Shabbos; she's always dressed and ready and by my side when I light the candles. She wouldn't miss your Shabbos table, your zemiros, even your d'var Torah that she doesn't always understand. But afterwards..."

Her courage seemed to desert her and she looked at him appealingly. "Don't you see, Leibel? Winter evenings *are long and there's nothing for her to do. She'd agreed to study with Jennifer; they're both determined to do well on their exams. She won't do anything...silly. She knows it's Shabbos. They just talk."*

*"Talk!" The sound exploded in the quiet room. "What's there to talk about? Again the books and the exams? My mother, who was more clever than any man I know, could barely write her name. Even in shul, she would have to sit behind the zoggerke."*

*Yehudis smiled gently, remembering old Mattel, the "zoggerke," who davened out loud, and all the ladies said the tefillah after her, word for word.*

*Leibel smiled too and his voice softened. "You know more than that, Yehudis," he said. "Your father was a kohen and a talmid chacham and he wanted his daughter to know how to daven. So you're able to teach her. She doesn't even have to go to school anymore; she's twelve and by law she only has to go to till age ten."*

*Yehudis shrugged. "In this area, Leibel," she said meaningfully, "people don't worry about that law. They don't have to send the older children to work in someone's kitchen so they can put food on the table for the little ones. They can afford the fees at the secondary school, and so can we for that matter, even if our house isn't as big as the ones on the Hill. Chaya'le knows that."*

*Judy saw her look around at the ornate room and sigh. Yehudis's thoughts echoed against the walls, plain as though they'd been spoken: Maybe things would have been different if Chaya'le had been a boy. Leibel would have learned with a son, and his old fire and fervor would have gone into building a better environment for him. Perhaps he would have fought the shul committee members who insisted that Jewish day education was only for the poor, or those that felt that the money was*

## Chapter Seven

*better spent on soup kitchens and housing for the flood of refugees from the Ukraine. But a girl? A girl, after all, had her mother to learn from, didn't she?*

*How could he understand that Chaya'le, or Vivian as they called her, cringed each time her mother entered the school yard and tried to speak to the teacher in her broken English? How could he understand that her friends and teachers spoke only about the new opportunities that were opening up around them, of Miss Buss at North London Collegiate School whose gates glittered before them like Pike's Peak to the Forty-Niners; a gold rush for the prospectors? Chaya'le knew, however, that to her parents it was forbidden gold, and the rivulet of resentment within her was growing into a stream.*

*Judy turned now toward Leibel. Had he, too, heard Yehudis's reverie? He sat quietly, and now it was his voice that shouted out through the room; his turbulent thoughts were audible.*

*The words* this area *had cut through Leibel like a kitchen knife through butter, and he couldn't reply. Had he made a mistake? He tried to find the words to say to Yehudis; he could see the tears beginning to form in her dark eyes that were focused on the Shabbos candles. Through her clouded vision, the flickering candles seemed to flare up and spread out, towards the white lace curtains at the window, towards the ceiling high above her, filling the room with a dancing yellow flame.*

*As Judy stood rooted to the threshold in horror, the invisible barrier, which always felt like a cold sheet of glass, suddenly became hot to her touch. She watched as the flames above the candles began to crackle and flare out uncontrollably, and from the distance, she could suddenly hear the harsh clanging of a bell mingling with the shouting of men and neighing of horses. She shut her eyes to the blazing brightness, but the flames still danced before her closed eyelids. For a moment, she tried to turn and run, to race upstairs to the safety of her sleeping bag, but she found herself running in place, her legs pumping beneath her twisted blanket as she shouted in her sleep.*

"Judy, wake up! It's only a dream."

As if from across an ocean, she could hear Penny anxiously calling her, shaking her, dragging her back from the sea of flames, but the pull from the front room was too strong to ignore. Petrified that she might lose the gossamer-thin connection to her dream, she pushed Penny's hand away in irritation. "Don't. I'm okay. Just leave me alone."

She vaguely heard Penny return to her bed and she waited to see what would happen. She knew that the double act was still on: the floorboards were stiff and hard beneath the wadding of her sleeping bag, but she knew she still stood at the barrier.

*Or were there two barriers in place now: one which prevented her from entering the front room, and one which held her imprisoned from behind, unable to climb the steps to safety. Judy put her hand out before her. She could feel the heat radiating outward like an electric heater on a cold winter night. Then she sensed that the flaring light was dimming, growing darker and shadowy as the clamor receded into the distance. Judy slowly opened her eyes again, expecting to see the cracked blue walls of the empty front room, but Yehudis was still there. Only this, Judy knew, was a different Yehudis, in a different time and place, a place very far from Kyverdale Road, a place and time that Yehudis was remembering as she stared into the Shabbos candles. The clangs of the firebell still resounded in her ears.*

## Chapter Eight

**F**IRE!

The discordant tones of the firebell clanged through the cracked shutter, echoing in the quiet room. Judy saw Yehudis look up from the pot she was stirring, ladle poised in her hand as if to ward off an impending disaster. Leibel was up and out of his seat in one quick movement, his chair scraping a path through the packed dirt floor. He threw the wooden door open and stood motionless on the threshold for an instant, his tall broad frame outlined by a shadowy light that seemed to dance across the village sky. Then he was off and running.

"Bolt the door!" he threw over his shoulder as he went. "There may be trouble."

Trouble? Judy thought. What kind of trouble? Why couldn't they just take care of the fire? Where were they, anyway?

Judy saw Yehudis shaking as she threw the rusty bolt firmly into place and hauled the heavy walnut bureau in front of the door for good measure. She went to the windows, making sure they were shut. For a moment Judy could see flitting shadows through the gaps in the spiky hedge that shielded the entire front window; people raced past, buckets clanking at their sides, and she tried to see *in which direction they were running. She could almost hear Yehudis reassure herself: They seem to be going towards the square, away from my parents' home, closer to where the Jewish quarter ends. Leibel's admonition rang in Yehudis's ears and she hurried to bolt the shutters, then went to check on the baby, peacefully asleep in the wicker cradle.* Judy knew this was Chaya'le. Now things were making sense.

*Yehudis tucked the baby's blanket more firmly into place. The child had long outgrown her swaddling clothes and now was rapidly filling out the cradle that they had borrowed from Mume Sheindel; they would soon have to put together a trundle bed for her. Just standing and watching the baby calmed Yehudis, yet at the same time filled her with dread. They were living through terrible times. What kind of future was there for Chaya'le?*

*She drew up the straight-backed chair to the fire and reached for her well-worn Tehillim. How many generations of women had poured out their hearts along with the tears that wet the pages before them. They cried for their husbands and sons, for their parents and children, but each teardrop became a tiny globule of liquid that magnified the letters it fell upon, as if to expand them into a* tefillah *that included all of* Klal Yisrael.

*Yehudis thought of her mother-in-law who could barely read the* tehillim, *but knew all of the* techinos *by heart. The older woman's tefillos were said in Yiddish, without any sefer before her, and her tears would fall into the giant vat of fats and lye that bubbled as she stirred all day, making the green household soap that she sold to support herself and her children. Many years ago, she had dreamed that her only son Leibel would become a* talmid chacham *like her grandfather and his father before him, who had been* Rav in Kiev.

## Chapter Eight

*Now Judy found herself tuned in to the thoughts of Yehudis's mother-in-law, reminiscing about her son. Leibel had been a bright little boy, absorbing the lessons he learned on the bench in the* melamed's *cottage, sopping it all up like a sponge, eagerly waiting for more. By the time he was fifteen, he was sitting in the little wooden shul most of the day, with his three good friends, Yoine the Rav's son, and Mechel and Shloime, both sons of the village shochet. How proud she had been when he told her that the Rav and Reb Simcha the Kohen would join them in their learning sessions before Minchah, and when Reb Simcha came to tell her that her son was a very special lad, she had nodded in firm conviction. Yes, I knew it all along. But the tears that she secretly cried when they left were not entirely tears of joy.*

*Once, she had dreamed of sending him to yeshiva, but she had to accept an unhappy fact of life: she needed him at home. Who would load the heavy wooden crates onto the cart each morning as she went off to the market to sell her soap? Time was passing and her daughters were growing up; it was time to think of a dowry. She couldn't go alone to the outlying villages in search of new customers, but Leibel could. She comforted herself knowing that before and between each journey, he could be found at his place in the shul, learning as well as he always had.*

*Then one terrible morning, the dreaded draft notice had arrived. Yoine was pale and anemic and Mechel had a club foot, but Shloime and Leibel were both tall and strong and they joined the group of village lads who did not have the money to bribe the inspector.*

*So Leibel joined the army. Four years is a very long time, but accompanied by his mother's tears and tefillos, he held his own through the rigorous training, trying to stay on the commanding officer's good side as much as possible.*

*And Hashem had helped. For some reason, the commander decided to place Leibel in charge of the supply procurement for all the army depots in the area. That job had put him in the driver's seat of the army supply cart for most of those four years. Which suited him fine, for the family that held one of the army supply contracts happened to be Jewish. That meant that twice a week, Leibel drove to their home in the village several miles down the river, where they filled the wagon with great round loaves of black bread. On Mondays they would load onto his cart long earthen pans of kosher roasted geese that had slowly browned in their oven, twenty-five at a time. So, once a week, and when the weather was cold, maybe the next two days as well, Leibel could eat the meat in the army kitchens along with the rest of the men. On those days, Leibel would eat his food slowly, chomping his meat loud enough to be heard by the commander, who was watching from his post at the corner. The rest of the week he would feign some stomach disorder and insist that he could only eat bread and vegetables. And each week, they believed him, remembering how noisily he'd eaten his goose.*

*In other battalions, though, the Jewish recruits were in for a difficult time. They would start off by eating the bread and potatoes, but that would very soon come to the attention of their fellow soldiers. They might try to explain that the meat was forbidden and that the rest of the food was enough for them, but they would only succeed in enraging the commander.*

*"Zhid!" he would shout. "Do you think I don't know what you're up to? It's a conspiracy! You are deliberately fasting and weakening yourselves. You are trying to un-*

## Chapter Eight

dermine the strength of the Czar's army!" And beatings would follow, along with forced feedings of their revolting stews.

"Leibel is an aristocrat," the men would laugh. "His stomach only tolerates roasted goose." And they never caught on to his tricks.

Best of all, Shloime was stationed nearby, all the way through, and the two boys continued their learning partnership as best they could. Four years later, when they finally returned to the village, Reb Simcha the Kohen took him as a son-in-law, as Yehudis became his wife.

Yehudis turned the pages of the Tehillim slowly, davening for her husband's safe return, for the safety of her parents in their cottage at the edge of the village, for peace in the little community. She looked around for a moment at the bare but pleasant cottage. Her Leibel was a coachman: "Leibel der hoicher" they called him. There were two coachmen in town and both were called Leibel, but her Leibel was the tall one. Her Leibel was also the one who only took jobs in the afternoon, even the ones that he did for his mother, because he insisted that his brain was freshest for learning in the morning. And in the afternoon, her Leibel said mishnayos by heart as he loaded his cart and fastened the harness.

The distant sounds and shouting had quieted and Yehudis looked up from her Tehillim. The shadowy light that had somehow penetrated the cracked wooden door and shutters slowly died down into the familiar late evening darkness. Boots and shoes are all soled in leather, Yehudis thought, but above the clumping of boots outside and the quiet voices of the villagers returning in groups from the scene of the fire, she could hear Leibel's distinctive tread and his voice raised in conversation with another man. Pushing the old bureau back into place, she hurried to unbolt the door before he'd even knocked. She might be slight, thought Judy, but she was strong.

The sharp acrid smell of burnt timber preceded the two men as they entered the small wooden cottage. Yehudis recognized Sarah Breindel's son, Itche, as he came through the door. Leibel was hot and sweating but Itche appeared comfortable, casually chewing the straw he always tucked into the gap between his front teeth.

"Baruch Hashem, it's out," Leibel said as he collapsed into the high-backed wooden chair at the table, stretching his long legs out before him. Yehudis looked at him sympathetically; it had been a long day and he hadn't even had his supper yet. She hurried over to the pot that still stood patiently by the fire and stirred it back to life.

Leibel looked up at Itche who was hesitating by the door.

"Why are you standing there like a hitching post without a horse?" he asked, patting the chair beside him. "Come, sit down, Itche. I haven't had my supper yet and I'm sure you haven't either. Set another place, Yehudis."

Yehudis saw the way Itche glanced around the small bare room, his quick eye taking in the old wooden table, the rickety chairs, the chipped enamel cups stacked neatly on the shelf above the fire.

"Don't worry, we have plenty," she said quietly, reading the thoughts that were running through his mind. "Have you already eaten at your mother's house?"

"No, I haven't," he reluctantly admitted, slowly drawing out the third chair at the table and perching himself on its very edge. "She doesn't even know I'm here. I've just arrived from Pereyaslav and I stopped to help at the fire. That's where we ran into each other." He clapped Leibel

## Chapter Eight

*affectionately on the back. "The two of us are never too far apart for long, are we?"*

*Yehudis had to admit that was true. The two of them had been born in this village and had played together in the mud puddles that formed where the cobblestones of the square had sunk down. They had sat together on the rickety bench in the* malamed's cottage *— but what a difference there was between them. Both Leibel and Itche were sharp enough, but unlike Leibel, Itche could never sit still. He was the one who let the field mouse run suddenly out of his sleeve onto the* melamed's table, *sending all the boys shrieking and scampering away. He played truant time and again, no matter how much his widowed mother cried and pleaded with him to go to school.*

*When Itche had been taken into the army his mother had cried again, remembering her twelve-year-old brother Velvel who had been snatched by the* khappers, *the dreaded trio of misfits who were shamefully hired by the village council to meet the government quota: twenty boys from the village for the Czar's army.*

*That was under Nicholas I and the Czar's army meant six years of training in small military cantons, followed by twenty-five years in the regular forces. Velvel was one of the lucky ones; a small group of Jewish boys had managed to stick together, reminding each other that they were Jews, even though their homes and families became just distant memories. Thirty-two years later, he had returned to his village, a full-grown adult, hardened by his army life, but determined to live among his fellow Jews.*

*Today, Velvel the water carrier was a familiar figure in the village as he walked his route each morning, his broad back bent under the weight of the buckets. Each night, after* ma'ariv, *he sat at the back of the shul during Reb Sender the Gabbai's Ein Ya'akov shiur, trying to understand the words, trying to stay awake. But he was happy to be alive, remembering Chaim'ke who had never survived the long march through the snow, Shimon who died on the front in the Crimea, and Moishe who was separated from them right at the beginning. Strangely, he'd run into him just two years before he'd come home, and all Moishe could talk about was the farm in Siberia the army had promised to grant him. He had never come back to his people.*

*But the army that Itche had been forced to join was the army of Alexander the Second. Only four years, they said, and Sarah Breindel was glad. Itche came back to her, took a wife and settled in Pereyaslav, but he was as restless as ever. He would spend his days shuttling between the villages, buying hides and wares from the farmers and villagers, haggling with the peasant women in their colorful head scarves, then selling to the townspeople who came in their sober grays and browns to buy what he brought them from the countryside.*

*Itche had kept contact with Leibel in the army too. He was right; they never had been separated for long. Even now, whenever he came to the village to visit his mother, or to buy another batch of soap from Leibel's mother, he would stop to talk to his friend in shul after minchah.*

*Yehudis ladled out bowls of steaming potato stew and piled sliced chunks of black bread onto a plate. Plain fare, but* baruch Hashem *plenty, she thought to herself. Meat sliced in threads was only for Shabbos, but potatoes grew behind the house in the little square of green that they called their garden. Yehudis boiled them and mashed them with a little milk, or grated them into latkes fried crisp and brown. Sometimes, when she had some, she cooked them with a bit of salt herring and a tablespoon of herring juice. Today, she had made a stew with onion and salt*

## Chapter Eight

and pepper, and even a few chunks of carrot and turnip; everything was there except the meat. Still, the steam rose invitingly from the dishes as the two men washed at the bucket in the corner and took their places again at the table. They made the berachah aloud, dipping the bread into salt, and Yehudis watched with satisfaction as they cleaned their plates, mopping up the last bit of sauce with the thick chunks of bread. Then she spoke quietly, finally daring to ask, "Where was it?"

"Chunye the tanner," Leibel replied briefly, blowing gently on the glass of hot tea his wife had set before him. "It must have been some dry straw left too near the fire in the tannery ovens."

Yehudis looked hopeful. "So it wasn't set. That's a relief at any rate."

"Relief!" Leibel laughed shortly. "And what about the police inspector who was strutting around like a rooster in front of the tannery tonight?"

"What do you mean?"

"Don't you see?" he asked patiently. "You're happy no drunkard from the tavern set it just to spite the filthy zhids, right?"

She nodded.

"So, you know no one else set it. And I know no one else set it, and all the Jews know that no one else set it, but this inspector is busy poking his nose into things now. He thinks Chunye set it."

"Chunye?! Whatever for?"

"Insurance."

Itche laughed bitterly. "Never mind that he isn't even insured; who has money for insurance in this town? Never mind that he was running around demented while his livelihood was going up in smoke. He didn't even join the bucket brigade. There we stood, all of us in a row, *frantically passing the heavy buckets back and forth from the well to the fire. And the men in the front were pouring water on the flames, trying to get that fire under control. And along came that idiot Krassofsky and accused Chunye of setting the fire!"*

"Did it spread anywhere?" Yehudis thought of the low thatched roof of the tanner's cottage, where the smallest of the village goats sometimes climbed to have a snack. Just next door lived her sister-in-law. She could imagine the scene in her garden as the geese she raised for their down ran amok in the face of the fire.

"Mirel is fine," Leibel reassured her, reading the fears that were imprinted soundlessly on her face. "But the tannery is gone." He sighed. "Insurance! Now those peasants will have what to talk about in the tavern for the next six weeks with Protopkin's henchmen egging them on."

"They have the system perfected down to the last detail," Itche commented. "First, Count Protopkin's spies buy the peasants some free drinks to loosen their tongues. Then, when they get all the complaints out of them and hear all about how the count bleeds them with taxes to spend on his parties, they tell them they've got their facts wrong. The count's an archangel who only wants their good. All the problems they have are caused by the Jews!"

He turned to Leibel in anger. "You wouldn't believe the rubbish they write in the papers in Kiev. Here, the peasants can't even read, but the lies filter down to them along the grapevine. Do you know what Purik the goose boy called after me last week when I passed him down by the river?"

"Purik? What can he say already?"

"You wouldn't believe it," he said. "He shouted, 'Hey

## Chapter Eight

Zhid! What did you put into the afikoman?'"

Leibel threw back his head and roared with laughter. "Afikoman? Where did he get that word from?"

Itche didn't laugh. "It isn't funny," he said seriously. "He got it from his elders. Think a minute, Leibel. The priests have been saying for hundreds of years that Jews put blood into matzah. Don't you see? They know about matzah shemurah; we guard it from when it is wheat in the fields. So they think there's something very suspicious about it all, and when some bright brain heard the word afikoman, he thought it sounded even better than ordinary matzah."

Yehudis listened quietly, not believing what she heard. How was it possible, she wondered, that Jews should be accused of drinking blood when they took such great pains to soak and salt their meat for hours to get every last drop of blood out of it? Just last week she had thrown out two precious eggs when she had found a blood spot on each one; would she mix blood into the matzah dough? It was ridiculous, but no one was laughing.

"And that's not all," Itche continued, his voice dropping to a whisper. "They're still hunting for the two sons of the count's coachman who went missing on Sunday. They were always playing near the marshes, at the turn of the river where the wooden bridge used to be. It's a dangerous spot, and I'm sure their bodies will wash up to shore by the end of the week, but meantime, you know what they're saying."

Yehudis did know. On her way to her parents' house the day before, she had passed the river where two washerwomen had been hard at work. The big peasant women had winked to each other as they pounded the sheets with their heavy wooden sticks, and she could hear Marusha comment as she passed, "If we'd put all those Zhids *in prison, we'd find out soon enough where Peter and Andriusha are. Mark my words!" And she'd nodded her head sagely.*

*Yehudis sighed. "Between the count's spies, the missing boys and now the fire, they've got three sticks to beat us with. So which will they choose?"*

*"Choose?" Itche snorted. "They cook it all together into one lethal brew and it all blows up in our faces!"*

CHAPTER NINE

Judy awoke with a start, perspiration oozing from every pore. She could hear her own heavy breathing in the silence of the room and realized it was still nighttime. Desperate to finish her dream, she willed herself back to sleep, replaying the final scenes in her mind. The images flickered like a dying flame as she struggled to recapture them. Soon she began to plummet once again into that other world, where Yehudis's thoughts became her own.

*It had started in the tavern the very next evening, with a little help from the village priest. Old Vladimir had dramatically called the villagers together for a "memorial service" for Peter and Andriusha. There he had eulogized the two innocent children, describing them as veritable saints, so beloved to their friends and neighbors, and all the peasants bowed their heads and wept. Even Mitchuk the cobbler, who only last week had chased the two rascals and threatened to drown them in the river when they had thrown a stone through his window, now sat and shook his head in sorrow.*

*"We all know who the murderers are!" the priest had thundered.*

*And all the people had nodded and muttered among*

*themselves, the whispers slowly growing into a shout, a malignant mystical chant: THE JEWS!*

*That had been early morning. By early evening, the streets of the Jewish quarter were deserted; all day long the tension had stretched across the village like a bank of thunderclouds massing for a storm, and as the daylight dimmed into dusk, people began to barricade themselves into their homes for the night. In the evening, the villagers, hot and thirsty from a long day's work, headed for the tavern for some liquid comfort. There they were joined by the farmers and peasants of the outlying areas, and as glasses of vodka were downed, the temperature went up to a fever pitch.*

*Yehudis could hear the birds rustling in the little nut tree outside, their wings whispering in the branches as they settled down for the night. She envied them their haven in their perch above the quiet street; a quiet that sent them off to sleep, instead of listening for the slightest footfall from behind the bolted door. Leibel too, had taken refuge, in the solid pages of the Gemara open on the table before him, the heavy iron poker lounging idly against his chair. The wicker cradle was hidden between her bed and the wall, the candlewick bedspread that covered the bed draped over the cradle as well, with just one corner folded back for air. Chaya'le slept peacefully, unaware of the anxiety that hung all around like a pall of smoke.*

*The tavern stood on the northern edge of the village; the Jewish quarter huddled on the opposite side, as if keeping its distance as best as it possibly could. Perhaps it was because of the deathly silence in the Jewish streets, but the noise from the tavern was so loud that night, that even Yehudis, in her house at the end of an outlying road, could hear a distant murmur, like thunder rolling in faraway hills. The sound clouded her brain all evening as she sat*

## Chapter Nine

*over her* Tehillim. *Then a sudden running footfall brought her up and alert and Leibel looked up from his* sefer.

"What's that?"

*The footsteps raced up their street, then stopped short under the nut tree as the thudding of boots in heavy pursuit resounded on the packed dirt road. They could hear a rustling in the hedge before their front window but the shutter was latched and they were afraid to open it even a crack to see outside; the fire was banked and low, but even the slightest line of light in the dark street outside could bring them unwanted attention. The heavy boots sounded closer and they could hear the shouting clearly now.*

"Where is he?"

"Which way did he go?"

"I saw him come out of the synagoga and run that way!"

"No, this way!"

*The babble of voices seemed to be coming closer and Leibel and Yehudis stood by the bolted door, uncertain what to do. They could hear the labored breathing of the stranger just under their front window; he seemed to be shifting a heavy burden as he crouched behind the evergreen hedge that spread its branches across the front of the house, right up to the front door. For a moment, they heard him edge towards the door, as if to knock, and then they could sense his hesitation.*

"They're after him," *Leibel whispered hoarsely.* "We've got to help him."

"Don't open the door!" *Yehudis pleaded.* "You don't even know who it is!"

*Leibel stood at the door, his tall frame bent over as he put his mouth to the crack.*

"Shema Yisrael?" *he mouthed into the night air, his*

*voice carrying only inches beyond the wood.*
*"Hashem Echad!" came the furtive reply.*

*The heavier footsteps sounded again, but they seemed to be receding down the road in the opposite direction and they hoped the men had gone. Judy winced as Leibel slowly eased the bolt open, trying not to let its usual grating sound echo down the street. In one quick motion, he pulled the door open a crack, then swiftly shut it behind the black-clad figure that slipped into the room, but not before the pale sliver of light had been seen by one drunkard who had somehow been left behind.*

*Things happened so quickly: one moment, they were standing by the door, trying to decide what to do, and the next, Leibel and the black-clad figure were straining at the door which was slowly, inexorably being pushed open from outside. Yehudis stood frozen in fright as a heavy, mud-covered boot came through the widening crack in the doorway, followed by a coarse red face. Her eyes widened as she recognized Anton the blacksmith, his face contorted with drink. How many times had she stood in his shop as a child, watching the gentle giant shoe the horses with an expert hand. He would wink at the children clustered in the doorway of the smithy, and purposely pump the bellows, laughing at their awed expressions as the flames shot high. And here he was, a different Anton, as if someone had poured his contents away and filled him with hate and fury.*

*Leibel held his powerful shoulders to the door, but the stranger was hampered by his long black cloak; Yehudis could not see his face or his hands as he heaved his back against the creaking wood. Adrenalin surged through her as her eyes darted around the room, looking for a weapon. Her eyes lighted on the polished brass candlesticks that*

## Chapter Nine

stood on the mantlepiece and she quickly seized one, lifting it high above the ugly head that was almost through the door.

The gleam of the candlestick as she swung it through the air startled the blacksmith and his head jerked up in surprise. That was all Leibel needed for a final push, and the next moment the door was shut and bolted. In the quiet room, all Yehudis could hear was the thumping of her heart and the heavy breathing of the two men. Then, thankfully, the unsteady footsteps of the blacksmith sounded on the front path, as he made his inebriated way to join his fellows.

They stood in a trance for a moment; then the black-clad figure came alive, a hand emerging from the dark folds to pull away his voluminous cloak.

"Itche!"

His small lithe body disentangled itself from the dark folds of material and he gently laid down the burden he was carrying beneath it, beside the open Gemara on the table. Yehudis gasped. It was the village sefer Torah.

"I don't like the way things look tonight," Itche said briefly. "I promised the Rav I'd get it to safety."

It was the only kosher sefer Torah in the village shul, but Yehudis knew that in fact, it belonged to her father. He had written it himself, letter by letter, line by line, throughout an entire year. She had been very small at the time, but she could still recall the elaborate preparations: the ink he had mixed, the straight sharp lines he had carefully marked in the parchment. Young as she was then, she had felt the special atmosphere in the room as he sat down to write, a quiet tefillah on his lips as he dipped the quill into the inkwell.

Her mother too, had been busy, with needle and thread. Yehudis would stand soundlessly at her side, watching *the delicate, almost invisible needle flash in and out, spinning behind it a golden thread. Occasionally, she would reach out a small shy finger and stroke the rich blue velvet. She had never seen such material. Her single Shabbos dress was made from simple homespun, made pretty with flowers embroidered by her mother's skillful hand. But for a sefer Torah, only the best would do.*

*Of course, a silver crown, like those adorning the sifrei Torah in Kiev's shul, or even a small silver breastplate, was out of the question. But her brother, Chananya, was also intent on making this sefer Torah special. Many years older than his little sister, he was already married and the father of three. He too had gifted hands; today he was a much sought after craftsman in Kiev, but at the time, he was still in the village, turning his skills to whatever would earn him a living. Now his art would adorn the sefer Torah; as his father wrote and his mother stitched, his nimble hands were fashioning the atzei chayim, the wooden rods onto which the parchment would be rolled. The shafts were made to size, as for any sefer Torah, but the handles that Chananya created were a genuine work of art. Each was thick and rounded, then twisted into a distinctive shape, like a flame above a candle. Intricate scrolling was carved into the wood, as fine and delicate as the embroidered crown on the velvet.*

Judy stood at the barrier, straining forward to see. She watched the emotions flit across Yehudis's face as she looked down at the *sefer Torah* that lay on her table, away from the *aron kodesh* that was its home. Judy had never seen or heard of a *sefer Torah*, but she sensed its holiness and could almost feel the warmth of the intricately carved wood.

"What do they want of us?" Itche said bitterly. "All we ask is a quiet corner somewhere to peacefully live out our

## Chapter Nine

lives with our families. So it's Jewish lives and Jewish families. Why should that bother them? Why do they hate us?"

"Itche," Leibel said gently. "Their hatred is the biggest favor Hashem ever did us; without it, we'd be sitting there now in that tavern with them, trying to fill an empty life with gallons of beer and vodka."

Itche looked up at his friend, a glimmer of understanding crossing his plain rugged face.

"Don't you see?" Leibel continued. "They push us away from them and we go back to where we are meant to be. Right here." He reached out a finger to touch the treasure that lay on the table before them. Thin threads of light from the banked fire shone on the gold letters, lovingly embroidered on the velvet mantle.

Itche sighed. "You're right, Leibel. But it's easier for you." He looked at the Gemara still open on the table. "As for me, wandering around all day among the peasants, with the hatred dripping from their smiles...I've had enough."

Leibel eyed him sadly. "Look at it this way, Itche," he said quietly. "If things would be reasonably good, the thought could enter our minds that this is where we're meant to be and Hashem has settled us in for a nice long stay. But when things are this bad, we know for sure that we haven't just been put down in the Ukraine and forgotten. Perhaps one day soon the cup of tears Hashem is collecting will finally overflow and He will take us out of here."

The fire sizzled quietly as they stood for a moment, lost in thought. Then Itche roused himself, picking up the cloak from where he'd thrown it over the back of the chair.

"You're not thinking of going back out?" Leibel asked in concern.

"I think I'd better," Itche said. He looked around the clean bare room and then lifted the sefer Torah gently. "I have a secure hiding place hollowed out behind my mother's chimney for goods that I haven't sold," he explained. "I promised the Rav I'd get this to safety and I was sure I still had time; it usually takes longer for the peasants to drink themselves under the table. Those few hoodlums who followed me must have come out early for some air, and seen me running."

He listened quietly at the door for a moment. The faint thunder of shouting and laughter still sounded in the distance, but the streets were quiet. "It seems safe enough right now," he said, as Leibel slowly unbolted the door. "Make sure you rebolt it, and move whatever furniture you have in front of the door and window. Who knows what will still happen tonight."

He paused for a moment with his hand on the doorknob. "I never thanked you for opening the door," he said with his old jaunty grin. "Not everyone would have done it. You probably saved my life."

He hesitated.

"Leibel," he finally said. "You know, when I said I'd had enough, I meant it literally. I'm getting out."

The next few words came out in a rush. "Even my mother doesn't know yet; Kiev is close to Pereyaslav and I've gone there to apply for a passport. Last week, it finally came through and I'm off to greener pastures."

"America?" Leibel whispered.

"No, England. Remember my cousin Sender who used to provide your sister with material for her feather ticks? He's got a big business now in London and he's written me that there's room for me there. So we're leaving everything behind and off we go."

Leibel looked serious for a moment. "Everything?" he

## Chapter Nine

*asked. "Even this?" He reached out and touched the* sefer Torah *that was hidden beneath Itche's cloak.*

*Itche laughed. "There are shuls in London too," he said lightly. He turned to go and then he stopped. "Seriously, Leibel. If you ever decide to follow me, I'll be happy to help you, like you helped me tonight. And if you need to pass through Pereyaslav on your way to Kiev, you can always use my house. It's a little shack alongside my wife's Uncle Zalman's house and he'll be glad to let you stay there."*

*His face sobered as he looked around the quiet room for a moment. "Don't think I didn't understand what you tried to tell me tonight," he said suddenly. "You've given me something to take with me...if I get out of this place in one piece."*

*"Tzeschem l'shalom," Leibel whispered as Itche slipped out the front door, "Go in peace. And may Hashem protect us all tonight."*

*Much later, Yehudis could hear the drunkards emerge from the tavern; the steady rumble of noise that had sounded all evening suddenly exploded into a raucous shout that crashed through the tense dark streets. Another full day would pass before she and Leibel dared to venture out and discover what those rampaging hordes had wrought that night. From neighbors they learned that the men had come out in straight long rows, as if arrayed for battle; only their unsteady gait set them apart from an army sent out on a mission. They divided into ranks of ten and fanned out through the streets, led by their generals, Piotrkov and Vissaronovitsch, whom everyone knew were in the pay of the Count. They had joined the peasants in their drink, but the smell of liquor that hung about the two men came from their soaking wet sleeves. While the farmers and villagers downed their vodka, they* had tossed theirs down their sleeves; they were stone sober and knew exactly what they were doing.

But the peasants had been too besotted to do much. They had held clubs in one hand and undrained glasses of drink in the other, and some had been too drunk to know which was which. The blows that they had aimed at the barricaded doors had been far too unsteady to inflict much damage and the only home they had managed to enter was Chaim Zalman's little hut; he and his family had taken shelter at the gabbai's house on the hill, knowing that his shack couldn't afford him much safety. Ten drunken farmers had stampeded in through the broken door, in their eagerness to lay hands on the Jews' fabled wealth, and had broken every stick of furniture in their effort to find it. They had slashed the meager bedding and tattered curtains, hoping to find the coins he must have squirreled away, but finally had staggered out to the street emptyhanded, leaving behind them a heap of rubble: shards of glass, broken furniture reduced to piles of kindling, and thousands of feathers that still floated through the dark streets.

The rest of the men had rolled uselessly in the packed dirt street, hollering their hate along with their tavern songs. Piotrkov and Vissaronovitsch had finally called off their troops in disgust. For the time being, they had had to content themselves with a few smashed windows and the pleasure of striking fear in the heart of every Jew in the village.

Yehudis could bear the suspense no longer; she had to see for herself that the family was safe.

A few shutters were halfway open as she and Leibel passed, as if ready to be slammed shut again at a moment's notice. Bluma was out with her twig broom,

## Chapter Nine

sweeping up the crystals of glass that were strewn in front of her home, mingled with the feathers from Chaim Zalman's hut next door. Scraps and sticks of wood, all that was left of his furniture, surrounded the corner house like a deformed hedge devoid of its leaves. Bluma nodded somberly as they greeted her, and went on with her work.

They went first to Leibel's mother, in her house at the edge of the village where the forests began. It was there that she went to tap the resin that gave her soaps their fragrant scent of pine. The soap vat stood empty now; it was dangerous to work with hot fats and lye when the little ones were about.

"Mirel came here with the children after the fire," she explained to Leibel and Yehudis, as they looked around the crowded room. "Their walls were singed from the flames and their whole house smells dreadfully from smoke. The children were coughing all the time. So baruch Hashem, she was with me these past few days; I was as grateful for her company as she was for mine."

Yehudis smiled at her nieces, the sweet young girls who were always busy at their mother's table sorting the feathers: one basket for the feathers, one for the down and one for the sticks. Now they stood about uncertainly, their hands twisting with unaccustomed idleness as they watched their younger siblings play.

"Where's Shimon?" Leibel looked around for his brother-in-law.

Mirel sighed. "He went off to Kiev the morning after the fire," she said, lowering her voice so the children wouldn't hear her. "We were finding things very difficult as it was and had been thinking of moving to the city. Then, during the fire, the gate of our yard was trampled by the crowd. There isn't a single goose left. So Shimon has gone to Kiev to see if we can make the move now, and after these past *few days I just can't wait to go. I'm trying to convince Mama to come too."*

Leibel raised an eyebrow. *"Sell soap in Kiev? And why is it better there than here? Do they love Jews more in the city?"*

*"Maybe not, but there's safety in numbers. There are hundreds and thousands of Jews in Kiev."*

The scene suddenly shifted. Leibel and Yehudis were in a different house now, seated at a rough wooden table with an elderly man, who Judy somehow knew was Reb Simcha, Yehudis's father.

*Yehudis was astounded to find that her father agreed.*

*"But it's quiet now, Papa,"* she protested. *"Don't you feel it's blown over? There wasn't a sound in the streets today."*

*Reb Simcha smiled wryly. "Well, today they're all feeling a bit ashamed of themselves. Those two little rascals turned up; did you hear?"*

*"No!"*

*"Yes. Just think. They held a memorial service for them and wept and wailed, and all the time those two creatures had been hiding in the next town. It seems that on Sunday morning, they'd ridden off on the count's best horse, and when it threw them and bolted, they were afraid to come home; they knew their father's strap would be waiting for them. What they didn't know was that the horse had returned to the stables and was safe and sound with his head in the feed bag. And the Jews were facing the beating instead."*

*He stroked Chaya'le's head as she sat quietly on her mother's lap. "So that excuse has blown over,"* he said somberly. *"But the next one won't be far behind. Chananya has asked us to stay with him and I'm thinking*

## Chapter Nine

*of going. And if I could,*" he added, "*I would go further.*"

"*Further?*" Leibel asked. "*You mean, like Itche?*"

"*So he told you?*" Reb Simcha asked. "*Yes, like Itche.*" He sighed. "*Sometimes I feel that on this journey through* galus, *Hashem decrees where we stop and where we get off. We* daven *each day that this be the final station before the end of the line, but perhaps we still have to travel through the Western countries. Maybe it's England that will be the last stop.*"

He looked at the young couple. "*I'm too old to travel and start again. But what about you?*"

He smiled sadly at their stunned faces. "*Think about it,*" Reb Simcha the Kohen advised. "*On your way home now, take a look at the white marks that Piotrkov has chalked on the Jewish homes for future reference, and think about it. This time it was a drunken hunt for property; next time they'll come for blood. But whatever you decide and wherever you go, may Hashem guard and protect you.*

Yevarechecha Hashem v'yishmerecha.
Ya'er Hashem panav elecha, v'yechuneika
Yisa Hashem panav elecha,
V'yasem l'cha shalom...shalom..."

CHAPTER TEN

Yevarechecha Hashem v'yishmerecha. *The words echoed in Judy's head as she stood at the door of the front room in the house on Kyverdale Road, still imprisoned between two invisible sheets of glass; one that did not allow her to enter and one that kept her from running away. For a moment she wondered when she would finally wake up and get up and out of her sleeping bag. Or was she doomed to be forever trapped in her dream?*

*The room spun about as the words of the* kohen *reverberated from wall to wall, creating a kaleidoscope of forms and figures. Shadowy shapes flashed before her eyes: trotting horses, wagons piled with trunks and boxes, puffing locomotives, steamship decks teeming with people. Then out of the muddle of images, two pinpricks of light emerged, steadily gaining strength and growing, until they found their position once again to flicker above the Shabbos candlesticks.*

Yevarechecha Hashem v'yishmerecha.

*There was Yehudis, Judy saw — not the Yehudis of that far-off village, but the one she recognized from the house on Kyverdale Road. Yehudis, shaking herself out of her reverie, fingered the brooch that was pinned to her*

Shabbos dress, the brooch that Leibel had ordered from the silversmith before Yom Tov to remind her of her father's blessing, the blessing of shalom, the blessing of peace.

Peace had come only temporarily to the village; the fuse was still lit, only the wick had been lengthened. Sporadic outbursts had sent still others fleeing to the city, but it took the assassination of the Czar, years later, to finally bring the explosion. The fires burned in their hometown and in all the surrounding areas, then raged through the streets of Pereyaslav and Kiev, and hundreds of towns and villages.

The little brooch flashed as Yehudis leaned forward, its silver image reflected in the polished brass of the candlesticks. She smiled sadly at their copper luster, remembering how she had bravely held one high over Anton's head as he'd tried to push his way into their house. Still, she somehow felt that an even greater act of courage was to light these candlesticks each week, welcoming in the Shabbos, here on Kyverdale Road.

A soft patter of footsteps outside was followed by a knock at the door. Yehudis rose quickly from her seat; Judy could smell the faint scent of pine and feel the swish of her skirt as she hurried past her into the hallway. The candles flickered for a moment as the front door opened and shut, and Leibel looked up, forcing a smile as Chaya'le came into the room.

"Good evening, Papa," she said awkwardly, standing stiffly, as if waiting for his rebuke.

"Good Shabbos, Chaya'le," he replied in measured tones.

Yehudis bustled into the room with a stout young woman dressed in black, breaking the stilted silence. "Martha's here," she said with a bright, cheery smile that did not quite reach her eyes. "John isn't back from his

## Chapter Ten

*afternoon off so she said she was glad to come. I'm ever so grateful, Martha."*

Martha bobbed a shy greeting towards Leibel. "The Missus asked me to walk Miss Vivian home," she explained, taking off her hat and gloves and placing them on the table. "And while I'm here, I might as well give you a hand."

She strode purposefully over to the fire and stoked it carefully with the poker, raking it a little so that the ashes fell through the grate into the ash pan below. She scooped up a measure of coal from the brightly polished coal scuttle that stood near the fireplace, and with a quick deft hand she spread the coals on the fire, watching with satisfaction as the freshly fed flames blazed up and began to dance merrily in the grate.

Yehudis removed the covering from a plate on the sideboard, and brought it to the table. The aroma of cinnamon, apples and poppy seeds wafted through the room as she placed generous slices of tart apple pie and fresh sweet challah onto a white linen napkin, and folded the corners together.

"Many thanks for your help, Martha," she said in her gentle voice, handing her the little packet.

"Many thanks you to you, Ma'am," Martha bobbed and smiled. "There's nothing like your hallah bread, I'm sure."

Yehudis winced as Martha picked up her gloves and her stylish plumed hat, an obvious castoff from her fashionable mistress. Yehudis couldn't bring herself to wear the feathered contraptions the ladies all wore on their heads. She could never look at a feather without remembering her nieces, and Chaim Zalman's shattered hut; no amount of pleading from Chaya'le could persuade her to wear more than a small dark ribbon or bow in her plain straw boater.

As the door shut behind Martha, Chaya'le came to

warm her hands before the fire. She looked taller than she had the first time Judy had seen her and she gazed into the flames with a pensive air.

Yehudis sank down into the armchair and patted the footstool before her. "Come, Chaya'le," she coaxed. "Bring me the Tzeinah U'reinah and we'll read a bit before you go to bed."

Judy watched the girl's back go rigid, then yield as she relented.

"Yes, Mama," she said tonelessly, and she walked over to the bookcase with small stiff steps.

The two flickering candles on the table bathed the room with a warm and steady light, radiating a glow of peace that spread from wall to wall. It enveloped the father as he sat by the table, his head bent over the sefer, and spread to the armchair, where the mother sat with her daughter; the petulant frown on the face of the child slowly relaxed into a contented smile.

As Judy watched the peaceful scene, she wished that she could finally break the hateful barrier and enter to share it. She pushed that wall before her as hard as she had pushed the wall behind, when she'd desperately tried to run from the terrible things she'd been forced to watch, but both were hard and unyielding; no amount of pressure helped.

"V'yasem l'cha shalom."

Reb Simcha the Kohen's voice echoed in the room once again as the Shabbos candles began to flicker in their last gasp for air, in the melted pool of wax in the hollow of the tall brass candlesticks. As their shadows danced on the walls, the scene behind the barrier slowly began to melt and fade into the soft cream stripes of the wallpaper. The candles finally sputtered and went out, leaving the room in darkness.

## Chapter Ten

With a sigh of relief, Judy felt the floorboards beneath her soften, as they seemed to melt away into the warmth of her sleeping bag. She knew she could open her eyes now, and see Penny peacefully sleeping beside her. In the morning, she could enter the front room at will, with no barrier blocking the way. But there was really no reason for her to do so. There was nothing there for her to see. The blank white blinds would stare mockingly from their perch before the window, with only the faded triangle of cream and wine wallpaper high above the mantlepiece remembering what she had seen.

*What she had seen...* The dreams she'd been having were so unlike any she'd ever had before, and they made her feel decidedly uneasy. She needed to get some fresh air and clear her head so that she could examine them rationally, if that were even possible! There was no question about it, Judy told herself: the entire experience was unnatural; other-worldly, one might say.

CHAPTER ELEVEN

"You sure you're okay, Ju?"

Penny eyed Judy with a worried frown as they trudged up the road towards the traffic lights. "You look like you've been through a riot or something."

Judy winced. A pogrom, more likely. She gave an exaggerated yawn. "Had a rotten night, Penny. I just couldn't fall asleep."

That was true enough, she mused. When she had finally gone back to bed, after Penny had called her, she had spent the rest of the night in her sleeping bag, same as Penny. But half her brain had stayed awake, down at the front room door. She'd been sure it was close to dawn by the time that strange invisible gate had finally opened to let her out, but a look at her watch had shocked her; she'd been trapped in her dream for barely half an hour. She'd begun to think her watch had stopped, then maybe the sun in its cycle too, for the night had seemed endless. Afterwards, as she lay sleeplessly in her sleeping bag, the visions danced in front of her closed eyelids. Call them nightmares, she thought, except that she'd been awake when she had them, and remained so for most of the night.

"A bit of martial music will do you good," Penny commented, observing her pale drawn face through narrowed eyes. "I've never seen the changing of the guards, have you? We missed it that time our school came up to London for the opening of Parliament."

She flipped open her trusty *Visitor's Guide to London*. "Now let's see. After it's over, we can make our way down to Trafalgar Square and then wander around Westminster, House of Lords, and all that," she added, squinting down at the map as she walked.

"Umhumm," Judy mumbled, concentrating on placing one leaden foot in front of the other. For some reason, she didn't want to go anywhere today. Just sitting at home seemed to be the best plan of action right now, feeling the way she did.

Penny gave her friend another anxious look as they entered the corner Marlboro shop to buy their travel card. "You sure you're okay, Ju?" she persisted.

Judy didn't answer. Her eyes were drawn to the shelves of cold drinks for sale: frosted cans of Coke, 7UP and ginger beer. A tall skinny man with a shock of red hair was standing unsteadily in front of the display, examining the label of a can of ginger beer with a bleary eye. He was clearly drunk, and seemed to be trying to get drunker; not that ginger beer would help him. As he held the can up in one shaky hand, Judy put her hands to her throat. A sudden sense of panic overwhelmed her and with a rush of movement, she turned and raced out of the little shop, leaving Penny gaping after her from the counter.

Judy leaned against the shop front, her chest heaving as she tried to catch her breath. Several people glanced at her curiously as they passed and she seemed to catch a malevolent gleam in each eye, stoking her panic instead of easing it. Just then, two skinheads turned the corner; the early morning light shone on their bald pates and glinted

## Chapter Eleven

off the multitude of earrings they had between them. Vague memories of neo-Nazi marches on the evening news flashed through Judy's mind, and another wave of panic threatened to engulf her.

Every time and place seems to have them, she thought suddenly, remembering the Russian tavern songs of last night, and her heart pounded with a strange, unreasoning fear.

A flash of black and white caught her attention, and she looked down the road to see two dark figures advancing down the road in her direction. For a moment, she thought they were twins; both were tall and dark and bearded, but their garb was entirely different. One man wore a black hat, with an ordinary suit and tie peering out from under his dark winter coat, while the other sported long white socks and wore a strange round fur hat on his head, like the merchant in a Rembrandt painting. They were speaking quietly to each other, gesticulating as they walked, and they passed Judy by without noticing her. But Judy felt her panic pass as they did, and she suddenly felt safer, having them nearby.

"Lots of weirdos around here, aren't there?"

Judy jumped at the sound of Penny's voice.

"Sure are," she agreed, watching the skinheads depart her range of vision.

But Penny had missed the skinheads; instead, she was doubtfully eyeing an approaching trio of black-clad figures, dressed much the same as the previous pair. Judy had to laugh.

Penny turned to her hopefully. "You feeling better, Ju?"

Judy swallowed hard. *Zhid!* in Russian sounded worse, she told herself. "Don't call me that," she said with sudden irritation.

"Why not?" Penny's eyes widened in sudden understanding. "Honestly, Judy," she gasped. "You didn't think I meant..." Her voice trailed off as she tried to find the right words to say.

"Sorry, Penny," Judy said hastily. "Of course, I didn't...It's just..." Her mind whirled. No, she didn't think and now that she thought, she didn't really mind. Judith. If not for her name she'd have spent the rest of her empty life in careless abandon, and never come near to the house on Kyverdale Road.

"Well, I don't call you *Pen*, do I?" she said lamely, after an awkward pause.

"No, I guess you don't." Penny eyed her with a puzzled frown. "Are you sure you're alright, Judy? You're acting funny today. Do you think you're up to a jaunt around town?"

"No, I'm really not sure," Judy finally admitted. "I'm beginning to think I should go back and let you go off on your own."

There. She'd actually said it. She was not in the mood to ride buses and trains and run from one tourist site to the other; she would rather follow one of those black-clad figures, obviously dressed in their best, to wherever they might be heading.

Another dark figure passed them and Penny peered at the strange black and white shawl that peeped from under his coat.

"I wonder what language they speak," she whispered to Judy, jabbing her lightly with her elbow. "Do you think these people know English?"

Judy shrugged, but the question stopped her short in her tracks. How many languages had she listened to all of last night; the blessing of Reb Simcha the *Kohen*, the long conversations, even the tavern songs bawled by

## Chapter Eleven

the drunken peasants. Which language did Yehudis and Leibel speak? She hardly thought they spoke the Queen's English between them, alone in private conversation. Yet she had understood every word that was said in their front room on Kyverdale Road and back in the village in the Ukraine. And, she recalled, she had entered their every thought, understanding it easily, as if it were printed above their heads in a bubble, like in a children's cartoon. How strange! What was happening to her? Am I going mad? she wondered. My mind is turning on me! What *did* happen last night, anyway?! Scenes from her dreams flitted past her eyes like dancing figures in a kinescope.

As her memory focused on the twinkling of the Shabbos candles, Judy came to a sudden decision. "Do you mind going off on your own?" she asked Penny. "I'm really feeling horrid and I think I'll go back to bed. Maybe when I get up, I'll finally get some work done," she lied.

Penny grinned wryly. "There's a couple of Whodunits in my backpack for when you get up," she laughed. "I have a feeling your project will still be waiting for you when you get home, and then you'll just do any old thing like I did when I was in school."

Judy smiled at her sheepishly. "Honestly, Penny. You don't mind?"

"No, Judy. Honest. Go get some rest." She stopped and looked at her anxiously. "You sure you don't mind staying on your own? Do you want me to go back with you?"

"I'll be fine, Penny. You go enjoy yourself."

"Sure?"

"Sure."

Penny turned to go. "Well, if you get lonely," she laughed over her shoulder. "You can always go borrow a cup of sugar."

Judy froze. "What made you say that, Penny?" she asked shakily.

Penny blinked at her friend in surprise. "Really, Judy. I just tossed off the first thing that came to my mind. Isn't that the classic thing to do when you want to knock on a neighbor's door?"

Judy felt silly, pasting deep meanings onto every single word. Still, it was strange. A cup of sugar. Maybe it was an idea.

Judy walked along the street, on her way to Kyverdale Road. The traffic seemed lighter today, and many of the shops were shuttered. An odd assortment of pedestrians passed her; old ladies with shopping carts hobbling by, harried mothers with children running for the bus, then families obviously dressed in their best, walking calmly along, oblivious to their surroundings.

A sudden gust of wind came around the corner, sending the street litter flying; cellophane wrappers and potato chip bags danced in the air for a moment and then disappeared. Judy looked up to find her vision clouded, as if she were trying to see through glasses that were steamed up in the cold.

For a moment, the sounds were the same. She could hear the heavy double-decker bus chug off, and someone run after it, shouting. Then an engine coughed to life and a motorcycle roared towards the traffic lights, but instead of a black leather jacket and bright blue helmet in a cloud of exhaust, Judy watched in amazement as a prim young man in a Norfolk jacket and trilby cycled stiffly down the road.

*The street sounds were all at once muffled, and a sudden neighing assailed her ears. Seconds before, a black taxi had chugged along behind a streamlined butcher's*

## Chapter Eleven

van, and now, in their place, blinkered black horses drew square dark cabs and carts down the dusty road.

A small delivery tricycle came up behind a hansom cab and scooted around it, its small stout driver puffing as he pumped along, clinging to the handlebars that protruded above each wheel. He seemed intent on getting ahead of the cab and his side wheels lifted as he swerved around it. The black mare neighed in alarm as the delivery box bumped into her view, and for a moment, it looked as if she would rear and run, but then she placidly continued on her way behind the intruder. Only the driver, perched on a high seat behind the horse, raised his whip in anger, his whiskers bristling on his red face, as he shouted after the boy, promising to give the young scallywag his just desserts. An elegant matron peered out of the cab window from under her elaborate plumed hat and clucked her disapproval. She turned her attention to the pavement beside the chipped stone street where Judy stood and, smiling graciously, she waved a white-gloved hand.

Judy blinked, then realized that the women beside her on the sidewalk were waving back. Where seconds before a stout matron in a short, garish pink raincoat had struggled to get on a bus, three young ladies strolled calmly along, slim white feathers nodding gracefuly above their heads, black bunched skirts trailing behind them. Tall grasses waved around the bean-shaped pond across the road and Judy could see a group of children playing with large round iron hoops.

"Here comes Vi with her wooden hoop," they chanted in derision, as a small dark girl in a thick navy cloak darted across the road before an oncoming mare broke into a canter.

Judy heard her childish voice raised above the rumble of the wooden cart wheels. "I'm not playing today," she *said defiantly, tossing her curls back from her face. "Only watching."*

"Nyaa, nyaa. Wooden head's got a wooden hoop. Vivian's always different!"

Judy watched to see what this smaller, young Chaya'le would do, but the mist that clouded her invisible glasses began to lift. She stepped back in alarm as a huge articulated truck thundered down the road, its numerous license plates flapping in derision as it passed her. The horses were gone, and in their place once again were lines of cars and trucks, punctuated by the big red buses that rolled towards the traffic lights.

Judy shook her head, as if to clear the wooliness from her brain and forced herself to go on. She had wondered last night if she would be forever trapped in her dream; was she sliding back into it now by day? Help! Had she no control whatsoever over her mind? Mum would be frantic with worry if I'd be home, she thought briefly. But, of course, none of this nightmarish hallucinating would have happened at home. She looked about fearfully, but the ordinary street around her stayed reassuringly the same. The scene that had played so clearly before her eyes had crumbled away into nothing, like the newspapers that had littered the front room on Kyverdale Road, and now everything was gone.

Everything?

Appearances can be deceiving. Judy thought about it as she walked along the road. Her favorite walk back home was on the beach along the Bill and she remembered the sunniest days on the shore, when she stood and looked out to sea. That's when she learned that sunshine doesn't always mean clear visibility.

Sometimes, the sun shines in a certain white bright-

## Chapter Eleven

ness, bleaching the sky to a thin pale blue, and creates a strange shimmering haze that hangs like a veil over the horizon. On such a day, as far as she can see to the east, the white flecked sky meets the white capped waves on a peaceful empty sea. Absolutely nothing for miles and miles. In actual fact though, that part of the sea is very far from empty. There is something hidden right there, although you can't see it when the sun shines in just that way. Judy knew, because she'd been there, that just a twenty minute boat ride away, in that direction, is a mass of land, an island, complete with cliffs and farmland: the Isle of Wight.

It's strange but it's true, something to do with atmospheric conditions and visibility that differ from day to day; one day the island is there, its every detail etched against the sky, and the next day it's gone, with only the horizon stretching its thin line between the sea and the sky. Strange that it is on a dimmer day, when the sun is shielded somewhat behind the clouds, or in the deeper blue of a stiller sky, that the massive island looms clearly on the horizon. Even the distant farmhouses are visible then, their roofs reflecting the sun, and at night you can see the strings of lights that mark the roads and populated street.

Judy thought of the scenes that melted in and out of the front room in the house on Kyverdale Road, just like the Isle of Wight back home. How much of what she had seen was still there, only obscured by some modern, blinding light? She thought of the two pinpricks of light that had grown into a window on another world, allowing her to step in and understand, then retreated back to their place above the Shabbos table. It was a dimmer light than the fluorescent light she was used to, but it let her see something that still lived and breathed, even when some people thought it had gone forever.

Judy shivered. She wondered, seriously this time, if she was losing her mind. Where were these curious images coming from? The names, expressions, settings and scenes were so very real! She'd always had vivid dreams, for as long as she could remember. But usually they'd been the result of falling asleep with a story line running through her head, like a bedtime story she'd told herself to while away the moments before she fell asleep. She had always been the type who lies awake after finishing a good book, imagining a hundred new and different endings to the story, what the heroine said and did for the next ten years or so. Sequels usually disappointed her; her own were so much better!

But this was different. How could she *know* all this stuff? she asked herself for the twentieth time. Not only was she conjuring up images of things she'd never experienced; she was hearing foreign words and phrases she'd never heard before — *and understanding them!*

A soft footstep sounded on the pavement before her and Judy looked up with a start as a young girl turned in to the path of the house just ahead. The girl was walking with that unmistakeable Shabbos step, the one that made everyone else look like they were running over the cliff. On a sudden impulse, Judy stopped to look where she had gone.

The door opened and shut behind her, and Judy only caught a glimpse of a hallway, with a flight of stairs leading upwards and a door opening off the side. Framed in that doorway were black and white figures, black-clad men wrapped in strange shawls like the one she had seen peeping out from under the passerby's coat. A snap at the downstairs window caught her attention and she saw that the shade had been pushed askew by a bright-

## Chapter Eleven

cheeked boy in a blue velvet brimless cap, allowing her to see inside.

As she watched, the sea of black and white parted all at once, she could see a tall bearded man in the center suddenly straighten, and with one swift strong movement he lifted something high above their heads. Judy gasped. A strange lump rose in her throat and unaccustomed tears suddenly pricked her eyes as she recognized the wooden handles that he lovingly held in his hands. These were round and smooth, rather than carved and pointed, but it was the golden warmth she remembered. Then a hand reached forward to straighten the windowshade and Judy was left outside on the pavement, staring at the blank façade of the house.

Judy plunged her hands into her pockets as she forced herself to go further. As she walked down Kyverdale Road, her fingertips touched the seams of her empty pockets and she twisted a loose string idly. Then, with a gasp, she suddenly realized that something was missing — her purse! She had left it in her backpack, beside her sleeping bag, and she had absolutely nothing with her. No wad of tissues that usually sat in her pocket, no money, and no key to get back into the house.

The bland white blinds at the window leered at her from the front of the house, as Judy stood and wondered what she should do.

"Anything wrong?"

A cheerful voice sounded from over the hedge, and Judy looked up to see the girl next door, standing in her front doorway.

"Oh, hello," she said shyly. She shifted awkwardly from one foot to the other. "I'm locked out, I'm afraid."

Malka looked concerned. "Where's your friend?"

"She went off touring for the day," Judy explained.

"We actually left together this morning. She locked up with her key while I went and left mine upstairs. Clever, aren't I?"

Malka laughed sympathetically. Then she brightened. "Bill has a key, doesn't he? But he's always out during the day, so there's no use calling him. Not that I could call him for you. It's Shabbos."

"You don't use the phone on Shabbos?"

"Nope. No phone. No car. No bell." She laughed the tinkly laugh that Judy remembered. "It's awfully peaceful."

Judy looked at her wistfully. Peaceful.

Malka eyed her reflectively. "Bill's usually home by five," she said. "And that's just right. Shabbos will be out by then. And you can stay in our place until he's back."

"Oh, no thank you," Judy said hastily. She heard a steady murmur from inside Malka's house and wondered if there were visitors. "I don't like to disturb you."

"Don't be silly," Malka said. "You're not going to stand outside in the cold all day, are you? Come on, join us. We're going to start our meal now and we have half a dozen visitors. One more won't even be noticed."

Judy looked pointedly down at the faded jeans that peeped out from under her anorak. "This visitor sure would be noticed," she said ruefully.

"No problem," Malka said cheerfully. "I'll give you something of mine if you're feeling self-conscious. Come on, stop arguing."

The guests were seated at the table and ready to eat when Judy came downstairs awkwardly, dressed in a woolen top and pleated skirt. She looked at the candlesticks standing on the massive tray in the center and was disappointed to see that they were empty, with only a wad of tired white wax to show that they had once been lit.

## Chapter Eleven

Somehow, though, the peace that she had felt radiating out of the lit candles last night seemed still to hover in the air as Malka's father lifted up the silver kiddush cup.

"*V'shamru b'nei Yisrael es ha-Shabbos...*"

Reb Simcha the *Kohen*'s voice resounded in her ears as Rabbi Fishman began, the blessing over the wine mingling with the blessing of peace: *V'yasem l'cha shalom.* It wasn't so much the words themselves that created the association, but the tone, the texture of the language that was at once strange and yet so very familiar...

Judy thought of the letters of the language, engraved on her silver brooch, and suddenly, she knew the answer to the mystery: Uncle Martin! Since she'd been a little girl, Uncle Martin had visited their home, regular as clockwork. He had no family of his own and so he'd made his niece's family his. And every time he came, he told Judy's mother stories he'd heard from "Granny Bess." Judy could see herself as a toddler, playing with her toys, as a five-year-old with her dollhouse, and as a ten-year-old with her nose in a book, while Uncle Martin spun his tales. She could not remember ever actively listening to him; she was always otherwise occupied. And in the past seven years she'd been almost too occupied to even say hello to him.

Somehow his stories had seeped into her subconscious, a vignette here, an anecdote there; the stuff of family lore. And then, in the house where much of it had taken place, the memories had floated to the surface. This explained so much! So, Judy thought with considerable relief, I'm not losing my mind after all! There were still a million unanswered questions, but at least now she had a hook to hang them on, something she knew was *real* and not the product of an overworked imagination...or something too spooky to contemplate.

CHAPTER TWELVE

Hebrew letters. Judy's thoughts had been far off, but now as she refocused on her surroundings, Hebrew letters swam into view. Everywhere she looked, she saw them. They stared up at her from the small square book near her plate, from the velvet covering at the head of the table, even from the framed wall hangings that hung between portraits of men with long beards. At first Judy felt as if she was being welcomed by familiar faces; she might not know their names, or even understand what they were saying, but they were friendly and they were smiling. But then she began to feel overwhelmed. The wall opposite her was lined with shelves from ceiling to floor and marching along them from end to end were books of every size and thickness; small and thin as a pamphlet, or tall and heavy enough to need two hands to hold them. All of them in Hebrew.

Judy felt like she'd been admiring a single crystal snowflake lazily drifting towards her from the sky, only to be overwhelmed by a blizzard. Who had time to read all these books, she wondered, and what on earth was written inside? The letters danced before her eyes, mocking her, and a faint irritation began to rise within her. She forced herself to look around the table instead, to see the people who crowded the room. Malka was right. One guest more did not make much of a difference.

"Do you always have this many visitors?" Judy asked Malka in an undertone, later, when she noticed that people at the table were conversing among themselves.

Malka smiled. "No. Sometimes we have more. And when my brothers are home from yeshiva, the place is really full!" She laughed to see Judy's face, then rose to follow Mrs. Fishman into the kitchen. "Come, let's give my mother a hand."

"Some of these visitors are regulars," Malka explained, as they carried the plates of steaming food through the hall to the dining room. "There's old Mr. Moss who's eaten here every Shabbos for the last ten years, ever since his wife died. Mrs. Malamud comes here every other week; we share her with her niece. Mr. Teppelman lets us know three weeks in advance when he wants to come, so my mother can make him her famous potato salad." They smiled at each other as they saw him reach over just then to take a generous helping, while Mrs. Fishman looked on with satisfaction.

"And the others?"

"The others? Well, Mr. and Mrs. Bender have just moved into this neighborhood, and my mother likes to invite newcomers. And then there's Misha and Irina." That was the young couple sitting opposite them. "They're on their way to Israel and they've stopped over in London. My father met them recently, when he was in Russia."

"Russia! What was he doing there?"

"Well, it's a long story."

Her hurried undertone stopped as they settled themselves back at the table. The conversation grew animated at the other end.

"Ukrainian Airlines makes a stopover in Lvov," Rabbi

## Chapter Twelve

Fishman was saying. "Not always, though. Sometimes they stop in another city instead, but I was lucky and it was direct from London."

"Long flight?"

"Not too bad. Just under three hours. It took me almost as long as that to get out of the airport and find Reb Shmuel's apartment. You know those council flats near the new road to Edgware, the ones that look like a sliced up checkerboard standing upright. That's what all the houses look like in the area. Row after row of faceless flats. It was like looking for one particular straw in a haystack."

Irina laughed. "And your streets here in London? They all look same to me. Winding around and around and you always come back to same place."

"Sorry." Rabbi Fishman grinned. "I guess it's a matter of what you're used to. But you're right. Nobody else seems to have difficulty finding Reb Shmuel's apartment. His living room is always crowded with people. People with questions and problems. Visitors from abroad who've come to see how they can help. And then the growing number of students who come to hear his *shiurim*, his lectures. Three times a day he gives them; two for beginners and one for the more advanced. And in between, there are more classes that his wife gives for ladies. It's unbelievable. Somehow he fit me in. I haven't seen him for years."

"Reb Shmuel is my father's cousin." Malka explained quietly to Judy, bending towards her as she spoke. "He's American and he and his wife are in Lvov, working with the Jewish community. They can come out in the open now, you know, now that the communists are more or less gone, and there's so much work to be done. They're even thinking of opening a school, like in some of the bigger cities."

"Did your father go to help him?"

"He wasn't really there long enough," Malka said. "He did give some lectures while he was there, and he brought them suitcases of stuff from London. Books. Kosher food. Other...well...things, that observant Jews need, and can't get there. But he went for something else. You see, Reb Shmuel had called him."

Her head jerked up as her mother gently shushed her. Her father was speaking, this time to the entire company. He spoke slowly and clearly, carefully choosing his words so that everyone at the table could understand. Even Judy.

"Ever been at a Shabbos table before?" Malka asked her later.

"No. Why do you ask?"

"I don't know. You don't seem to find everything completely alien, like a lot of first-timers do. I just wondered how new you were to all this."

Judy was saved from answering by the burst of song from the men at the table. It was true; she felt so comfortable in this room. So much of what she'd seen and heard this week had helped her to understand, but she couldn't quite explain that to Malka.

"Your father isn't American, is he?" she asked Malka quietly when the song was over.

"Yes, he is." Malka smiled. "His accent has more or less disappeared by now, hasn't it? His family was originally from Russia, though. His grandparents came over with the flood of refugees in the early 1900's and settled on New York's lower East Side. Ever hear of London's East End?"

Judy swallowed. "Yes."

"Funny how it was the same in America. Jewish

## Chapter Twelve

refugees settled here in the East End and there on the East Side. Maybe because they're both near the ports. You know, get off the boat and look for the very first room to rent. And both went the same way. Either they moved to fancier neighborhoods as soon as they could, or their children did, and left their religion behind them. Or they stayed there a little longer and eventually built up religious areas in other places. But with a lot of hard work. It wasn't easy."

"And your mother?"

"My mother's English. Born here. *Her* mother came over from Poland after the war. My grandfather made it here before the war. He came on a *Kindertransport* from Germany."

"Jewish people sure move around a lot," Judy commented wryly.

"Well, the ones who didn't were killed." Malka said bluntly. She pretended not to see Judy's cheeks grow pink. "Or look what happened to Irina's family," she added. "They stayed in Russia. Managed to survive the pogroms, and somehow even the Nazis. But Stalin killed her grandfather simply for having a beard and keeping Shabbos. Her parents were afraid to teach their children anything about being Jewish. So they didn't. That's why Irina has to learn everything now. And she's one of the lucky ones. She's making the effort to learn what she's missed. Most of those children who were never taught probably won't."

Judy looked uncomfortable. "Like me?"

This time, Malka blushed. "I didn't say that, Judy. You have to find out if you're missing something in the first place, don't you?"

"I guess so."

Judy was quiet the rest of the meal, sitting and absorbing the sights and sounds around her like a sponge. It proved to be a really wonderful day with so many new experiences that Judy felt she had to digest it all, along with the scrumptious food Malka's mother served. Even the small quick meal towards the end of the day was a time of togetherness and beautiful songs. And stories. Stories of people and places, and profound insights that made you think. Sometimes, the insight came without the story; it was just a thought on a Biblical verse and Judy enjoyed those too.

Best of all, not once did Judy feel like a stranger at the wrong wedding. It all felt so familiar, like the fresh sliced challah sprinkled with poppy seeds and the spicy apple pie they served for dessert. Only this time, she was actually tasting it, and not having to make do with a bit of fragrance wafting towards her, as she stood in the doorway.

Between the two meals, Judy spent a quiet afternoon with Malka. Even their ordinary talk was interesting. She would have thought she'd be bored to tears. Instead, she was surprised at how much they had to talk about; their different schools, their families, and their plans for next year. Malka was planning to study away from home in something she called a *sem*; her older sister was there now and she regaled Judy with tales of a life in a dormitory with a collection of foreigners from every continent. Between the giggles, Judy thought of the train journey that Reb Simcha the *Kohen* had described. There didn't seem to be a single station along the way where some Jew had not been told to get off.

At one point, Malka finally got up the nerve to ask that all important question. "What on earth are the two of you doing on Kyverdale Road?"

There was no way that Judy could brush her off with

## Chapter Twelve

an explanation about her coursework. Even if it were really the honest truth. Somehow, the whole story came out: her project, her plans, her uncle, and the small silver brooch with the Hebrew lettering.

"You can't read Hebrew at all?" Malka wondered. "Even to recognize the alphabet?"

Judy hesitated. "Well, I can recognize the alphabet, I guess. Or rather, I know when something is in Hebrew, and not Japanese." She thought of the biscuit wrapper. "But this is all swirly, you see. Really beautifully made. And there are, well, hands on it too. It doesn't just have lettering."

"Hands?" Malka was interested. "What do you mean?"

"Hands. In a certain position. Like a, like a *kohen*," the syllables were uncertain on her tongue even though they rang clearly in her mind. "You know, the blessing of the *kohen*."

"Really? And it goes back almost a hundred years? I wonder where it comes from. Who do you think was the *kohen*; your grandmother's husband or father?"

Judy was silent. Her father, she'd almost said, but she'd stopped herself in time. She wondered what Malka would say if she could describe Reb Simcha the *Kohen*, how he looked and spoke, the way he patted the baby's head as she sat on her mother's lap near the rough wooden table. But he wasn't the one who had given Yehudis the brooch. That had been made here in London, ordered by Leibel, and Judy still wasn't clear when. In memory of her father's blessing, Yehudis had said. Did that mean when he was no longer alive? It was strange how much she knew about Yehudis and Leibel, and yet how very little. But how much of what she thought she knew was from Uncle Martin's stories, and how much was dream-fantasy?

A sudden thought shook her. The letters. L. Schumacher. Was that L. for Leibel? 1903. It made sense. What those letters and clippings could tell her, if only she could read them. She eyed Malka doubtfully for a moment. She felt so close to her now, and yet, when it came to sharing that bundle she'd hidden beneath her sleeping bag, she felt exposed, as if someone was peeling off the front of her house while she was still inside.

"Malka, I wonder..." Her voice came out in a croak when she finally summoned up the courage to speak. "Do you read Hebrew properly? I mean really read it — if someone wrote it in a letter. Or a newspaper."

Malka stared at her, bewildered at the sudden change of subject. "I think so," she said uncertainly. "I mean, I can understand the Hebrew in my prayers very well, and the, um, books that we learn in. My spoken Hebrew isn't too bad, though I'm not very good at the idiomatic, modern Hebrew. That would make an Israeli newspaper hard for me to follow. Is that what you mean?"

Judy hesitated. "I don't know. I mean, the newspaper I'm talking about is a very old one, so I don't know how modern the Hebrew would be."

Malka stared at her. "Very old? How old do you mean? Ten years? Twenty?"

Judy took a deep breath. "No. Eighty."

"Eighty?" Malka squeaked. "Where on earth have you seen a newspaper eighty years old?" Her eyes widened. "Judy," she breathed. "You haven't found anything in the house, have you?"

Judy nodded dumbly. "Bill did," she finally brought out. "When he climbed into the loft. There was some other junk, and some coins that I think are also junk. But there's one packet I think would be interesting. Newspaper clippings dated 1903. 1905. And letters."

## Chapter Twelve

"Letters!" Malka leaned forward in excitement. "Names? Dates?"

"I really don't know." Judy shrugged hopelessly. "If only I could read them. I've hidden the whole bundle," she continued in a rush. "I don't know why, but I didn't want to share it with Penny. So I haven't had a chance to really examine it and see if I could make heads or tails of it all. Do you think you can read something like that?"

"I'd love to try. You sure it's Hebrew?"

"What else could it be?"

"Yiddish."

Yiddish. The word rang a faint bell in her mind. She remembered a long-ago birthday in Ilford; Granny Bess had spoken to Grandad in a strange tongue over her head, so she wouldn't understand. Later her mother had told her it was Yiddish. A language just for the Jewish people, she knew. She'd never heard it spoken by anyone else.

"Is there really such a thing as a Yiddish newspaper?"

Malka laughed. "Sure. And probably more likely than a Hebrew one, eighty years ago. Problem is, I'm ashamed to say I'm not very good at reading Yiddish, even though I speak and understand it reasonably well. I usually end up getting all confused when I read it. Still, I could try." Her eyes sparkled. "Ooo, Judy, this is fantastic. You know what? When Bill comes home tonight with the key, I'll come along and you'll show me the papers." She eyed Judy carefully. "If that's alright with you."

Judy smiled in sudden relief. "Alright? It's wonderful. Let's just hope that Penny's still busy somewhere and doesn't get home too soon."

The winter sun sets early in London and Judy had missed seeing the candles burning at the Friday night meal. But after nightfall, there was still one flame to be lit that she hadn't known about. The fragrant smell of spices mingled with the scent of wine and the scratched sulphur match that lit a tall braided candle, held high in Malka's hand. Later, Malka translated the words her father intoned: "*Ha-mavdil bein kodesh l'chol, bein or l'choshech, bein Yisrael la-amim...*

"Hashem has set us apart," she explained, "in exactly the same way that He set a barrier between night and day, and the days of the week and Shabbos. Our life is meant to be different and we've got the Torah to show us how."

She didn't say much more than that, but she didn't have to; Judy had heard these words from Leibel when he chided Itche. She remembered the beautiful pointed handles on the *sefer Torah*; the way the scroll had been held with such love in the village back in the Ukraine, and the way another man had held yet a different scroll, in the little shul down the road that she'd passed. She knew exactly what Malka meant.

She recalled as well the large open book on the rough wooden table that had traveled with Leibel and Yehudis to the well furnished room on Kyverdale Road. It looked much the same as the tall volumes that filled the middle shelf in Malka's dining room, the ones that Rabbi Fishman had studied from during the afternoon. She had watched him for a moment, as he sat by the massive dining room table, and she realized that reading was the wrong word to use. She remembered how Itche had envied Leibel his ability to find refuge in the pages before him, and how Yehudis had held her thick little book with much the same result. Judy took another look at the letters on the wall; they were no longer mocking, but challenging her. In a strange way she wasn't sure which

## Chapter Twelve

feeling disturbed her more.

Afterwards, they went into the kitchen to make that call to Bill. Malka paused with her hand on the telephone receiver.

"You sure you don't want to stick around a bit longer?" she asked. "Maybe you can come back here later, after Penny is back. We're setting up soon for tonight's lecture, and I'm sure you'd enjoy it."

For a moment, Judy was tempted to stay. She felt as if she were standing on the beach at low tide, tentatively poking one toe into a rippling wave that lapped at the sand. Here, it was still shallow and she was beginning to wade in, yet she realized that she needed to take a deep breath before entering the deeper waters.

So she shook her head and Malka dialed Bill's number. A square white book sat on the telephone table and Judy opened it idly, riffling through the pages. It seemed to be a history book of some sort, complete with diagrams and illustrations, and one word leaped out and caught her attention: *the Ukraine*. Straightening the book, she examined the full page map with branched arrows drawn across it. Judy took in the base and the ends of the arrows, the land where they began and the countries they stretched across and then she understood. This was the road map that Reb Simcha the *Kohen* had described; the route that the train journey followed over the generations.

Malka finished her conversation with Bill and, as she replaced the receiver, she smiled to see Judy engrossed in the book.

"Planning an A on your history GCSE?" Malka grinned.

"Actually, I am," Judy answered. "But it's not easy. I'm no history buff." She turned the book over in her hand, then she added thoughtfully. "But this stuff is different, isn't it? It's ours."

Malka nodded. She watched Judy flip through the pages again.

"Want to borrow it?" she offered. "You might enjoy it more than Penny's Whodunits."

The two girls laughed but Judy tucked the book under her arm, and when Bill finally came with the key, it went along with them, back to the empty house next door.

## Chapter Thirteen

The key grated noisily in the lock and echoed down the dark quiet street, as Bill swung the door open. "There you go," he grinned, and bowed them in like a butler. "Mind you don't do that again, Miss. It's awfully cold now to be standing outside without a key."

"Thanks ever so much," Judy smiled, and she shut and locked the door after he left. Malka looked about her nervously as Judy switched on the light.

"Aren't you frightened to be here on your own?" she asked, staring up the dark incline of the staircase.

Judy smiled. "I really don't know why, but I'm not." She peeked into the front room door as they passed it, its silence a welcoming homey one, as if winking to her over the secret that only the two of them knew; she and the front room and no one else. For a moment, she regretted bringing Malka here with her. Then Malka put her hand up to the peeling doorpost.

"There was a mezuzah here, once upon a time, Judy," she said quietly. "That's a little box with a parchment scroll of Bible verses inside, just like on our doorpost. That means a Jewish family once lived here, for sure. Take a look — can you see the marks?"

Judy looked and a warm glow filled her as she realized

that Malka was right. She knew she was doing the right thing. It was time to share.

The two girls went down the sagging steps to the little kitchen. Judy switched on that light too and pulled out the orange crate with a flourish. "Have a seat in my humble abode," she bowed. "Make yourself at home."

Malka giggled as she perched herself on the wooden box. "Come on, Judy. Let's get on with it. I keep worrying that Penny will come back and you'll have to leave it again for another time."

Judy took the stairs two at a time as she went up to the small dark bedroom and unearthed the bundle of papers. She could feel a thin layer of dust lining the pocket of the rucksack, where the outer paper had shredded into it. For so many years, the packet had lain undisturbed in the corner of the loft and now it crumbled with every delicate touch. Judy went down the steps carefully, holding the bundle gingerly before her like a tray of eggs, and deposited it gently onto the kitchen table. Malka watched quietly as she reshuffled the envelopes, waiting for her to make the first move.

"The stamps have been removed," Judy explained. "Neatly cut off, like for a collection. And there's no date. Just the address. See?"

Malka took the proffered envelope and turned it over carefully. "L. Schumacher," she read. "Name mean anything to you?"

Judy hesitated. She was certain she knew what the initial stood for, but then again, how could she ever be sure? "Never heard of it," she shrugged. "Let's try the inside."

Judy found herself holding her breath as Malka slipped the letter out and began to read. A frowning crease formed on her forehead as she tried to decipher

## Chapter Thirteen

the spidery handwriting. Judy watched her eyes travel ever so slowly across the first line, stopping at every letter as if trying to unscramble an anagram.

"This is not going to be easy, Judy," she said. "The handwriting is that old-fashioned spiky kind, not the well-rounded letters we use today. I can't even make out the date. I think the letter's in Yiddish, though. And the first words, even I can read. *To my dear...*"

Her eyes lit up and she looked up at Judy, excitement written across her face. "You did say her name was Yehudis, didn't you, Judy?"

Judy felt her heart leap violently and begin to pound in her chest as she struggled to keep her face calm. "That's what Uncle Martin said," she quavered. "Why? What does it say?"

Malka began again, taking a deep breath. "*To my dear Yehudis and Leibel.*" She looked up at Judy, and their eyes met. "Well, there you have the letter *L.*"

So that was their name. Schumacher. Of course, she wouldn't recognize it. Yehudis and Leibel had only one child, a daughter, named Chaya'le, and that was Granny Vi. When she got married, her name changed from Schumacher to Simons. *Her* son was Uncle Martin Simons.

Malka watched her curiously for a moment and then went back to the letter. The frown on her forehead deepened and Judy saw her gaze flit back and forth across the page in frustration, until she finally gave up.

"It's no use, Judy," she finally admitted. "It's like trying to break a secret code. I can't even make out which letter is which; it's such a flourishy scrawl. Are they all the same? Should we try another?"

For the next few moments, the only sound in the quiet house was the shuffling of papers, as Judy slowly withdrew the letters one by one and handed them to

Malka for her inspection.

"Nothing at all?" she asked after a while, her disappointment mirrored by the frustration on Malka's face. "What about the signatures? Can you recognize any more names?"

"I don't think so," Malka said unhappily. "All I can see is a string of words. Maybe the writer doesn't even sign his name. Maybe he writes: *Your father who misses you.* Or something like that." She pointed to the second set of letters that Judy had found; the one with the different handwriting. "This one's a bit clearer, and I think..." She jumped. "What was that?"

The two girls listened intently as the knocking sounded again.

"I think that's from your house, Malka," Judy said after a moment. "Sounds like a hammer."

"You're right," Malka smiled in relief. "I see my father has finally gotten around to fixing that broken curtain rod."

Judy fingered the rest of the papers restlessly. "We'd better get on with this before Penny gets back," she said again. "Maybe we should stop with the letters and try the newspaper clippings."

They put the envelopes carefully aside and, heads together, they shuffled through the yellowed pages covered with clear square print. As if by some simultaneous reflex, they stopped suddenly when they came to the photographs that Judy had seen before.

"What on earth is this?" Malka wondered. She squinted at the words printed beneath, trying to interpret the Yiddish caption.

Judy's eyes widened as she gazed at the yellowing paper for a second time. She felt as if she had been staring at a picture that made no sense, until someone handed

## Chapter Thirteen

her specially tinted glasses and the scene in the hidden picture sprang forward in perfect three-dimension. In her mind's eye, she stood once again in front of Chaim Zalman's hut, where the sticks of his furniture mingled with crystals of glass, and feathers blew everywhere, urged on by Bluma's broom.

"It says something about furniture being smashed," Malka said, thoroughly bewildered.

"It's a pogrom." Judy said quietly, a catch in her voice. "And look at this one." Judy felt a lump rising in her throat as the tattered bolts of fabric she had seen, when she last looked at this photo, were suddenly painfully transformed before her eyes into precious *sifrei Torah*, shredded by a mob. Now she could clearly make out the black script inked onto the parchment in sure straight lines.

"*Sifrei Torah* desecrated by the mob in Kishinev," Malka read. She turned to Judy as comprehension dawned. "We just learned about that in History. The big pogrom in 1903. I thought you said you're no history buff, Judy. How did you know so fast what this is?"

Judy shifted uncomfortably under Malka's curious gaze. "Oh, I don't know. My great-uncle once mentioned it, I think. What about the actual articles? Can you understand any of them?"

Malka stared at her a moment and then went back to shuffling through the pile; more clippings and some small square pamphlets, all in Yiddish.

"I don't know. It will take me ages."

Her fingers stopped suddenly and her hand jerked as she quickly extracted a neatly folded paper.

"English!"

It was several papers in fact, folded into each other all the way at the bottom of the pile, as if placed there by someone who preferred to read the Yiddish and left these for last.

"'Darkest Russia. A Record of Persecution.'" Malka read. "Seems to have been published here in London. Look at the price. One penny. Newspaper? Newssheet? The writing is tiny."

Judy read the paragraph beneath the masthead. "'This paper is published periodically with the object of bringing to the knowledge of the civilized world authentic facts relating to the situation in Russia.' Some mouthful. Rather understated, don't you think? No screaming headlines." She gingerly opened the large folded sheets. "All tiny letters. No bold print. Who bothered to read it?"

"How about this one?" Malka said, holding up the folded sheet beneath it. "Maybe it's more interesting. It even has a pink cover."

"Seems to be a newspaper, though," Judy said with a puzzled frown. "Isn't the Chronicle still published today? But look at this front page news!"

Their laughter was strained and slightly hysterical; it had to be. They assumed that somewhere inside news of the most awful kind must be buried, yet the cover was spread gaily with big bold letters: "*Have you tried the new product: MARMITE!*"

The next two pages weren't much better. Somehow, they doubted that Yehudis had kept this particular newspaper edition for the advertisement on the inside cover: "*Leveson's invalid chairs, spinal couches and carriages,*" complete with fine line drawings of all sorts of wicker contraptions. Or had she treasured the Personal Notices on the second page, with three columns under three separate headings: Births, Deaths, and Engagements. It was only on the fifth page, after the table of contents on page four, that they finally found the news: page after page

## Chapter Thirteen

of fine print divided into two broad columns. Their eyes skimmed the page and then homed in on one heading, as if it were outlined in the brightest red. Malka read aloud:

> The Outrages on the Jews at Kishineff, from our correspondent.
>
> Since the publication of articles of a certain tenor concerning the Jews in Bessarabetz, Nowozi Wremja and Swet, the people of our town commenced to display a hostile attitude to the Jews and openly expressed their disposition to settle their accounts with them.

"What polite double talk," Judy snorted. "'Of a certain tenor.' Sounds ever so gentlemanly, wouldn't you say?"

"Anti-Semitic ravings, probably," Malka agreed. "The Czar supported these publications, you know. It helped keep the peace in the country. Kept the miserable population from revolting against him; that would only come later. Right now, the newspapers were all telling them that everything wrong in Russia was the fault of the Jews. They're such horrible people, these Jews, that they even put blood into their matzahs." She pointed to the date, not noticing how pale Judy had gone. "See, it's Easter. That's round about Pesach time. Always a dangerous month for the Jews. Just look at this," she continued. "'*Settle accounts.*' Sounds like they're taking them to court. Ha."

The tone of the article changed suddely, the girls found, with the very next paragraph:

> Neither words nor pens can be found to adequately describe all that took place in our town on the 19th, 20th and 21st. At first the disturbers of the peace were only two or three in number but then they were joined by some twenty to thirty young fellows who threw stones, which they carried in their pockets, at the windows. The police seized a few of the youngsters but were obliged to release them owing to the threatening attitude of the older men.
>
> Easter came. All the shops were closed and a festive

149

> stillness reigned everywhere. Crowds gathered near the town center, seeking refreshment. Suddenly at noon, the surging multitude broke loose. "Throw out the Jewish brood!" came a shout. Exclamations of "Hurrah Hurrah!" broke from the throats of thousands of half-drunken individuals. Every Jew who was encountered was beaten until he lost consciousness. One Jew was dragged under a tramcar and smashed to death.
>
> The miserable dwellings of the poor were rifled of their contents which were removed into the street and piled into a heap. Immense clouds of feathers rose in the air.
>
> The Jewish hospital is packed with the injured. I saw one man....

"I don't think I can read more of this," Malka faltered. "It's awful. And listen to this:"

> In the Gostinaja Street, the synagogue was desecrated. Scrolls of Law were torn to shreds and thrown into the street. The police looked on calmly.

The police looked on calmly. Judy tried to imagine a mob running wild in London. They wouldn't be urged on by the government, like they were in Russia, and the police probably would do their best. But how much could they do if some football rowdies took it into their heads to go for the Jews instead? The *kohen*'s blessing suddenly rang in her ears: *V'yasem l'cha shalom.* She had never realized before how all important that blessing was. No news is good news, her mother always said, and it sounded so boring. What blessed boredom, she thought, to live a normal, peaceful life, day after day, surrounded by family and friends. Not looking over your shoulder as a leaf rustles on the path behind you, nervously listening for the sound of a mob approaching.

"So that's the photograph," Malka finally whispered, her eyes wide in her white face. "The *sifrei Torah.*"

"Both pictures," Judy agreed numbly. "The furniture

## Chapter Thirteen

too. Only the way this fellow writes, you don't need any photographs, never mind television cameras. You can imagine it all happening in front of you."

Malka's hand shook slightly as she turned the page. "Look," she said suddenly, pointing to an article further on. "It looks like this was circled. Either the ink faded, or it was faint to begin with."

> Threatened Expulsion of Jews from Kieff: Reuter reports that Kieff police are about to expel paviors, navvies, masons, carpenters, and whitewashers. It is estimated poor Jewish families numbering several thousand have left the town.

"I don't even know what half those craftsmen are," Malks commented. "Any idea?"

Judy was silent. Why did Yehudis save these pages? she wondered. Why was she torturing herself with what she had left behind? Her family had fled to Kiev; the word *carpenter* sprang out from the paper. Had she been looking for information that her family had never written, things that would never get past the censor? It was like finding fragments of a puzzle and wondering if you could still make out the picture, even though so many pieces were missing. She turned back to the original article.

"*From our correspondent*," Judy read. "Funny how we use the same word now even though it was more accurate then, wasn't it? I mean, in those days, they actually sent the news in written letters, delivered by courier, or telegraphed. It was definitely not called in by satellite!" She paused for a moment.

"You know, this is unbelievable," she continued reflectively. "Do you realize that all this took place at a time when there were reporters and newspapers and everyone sat back and read about it, and just let it all happen?"

"You are so naive, Judy," Malka smiled grimly. "And

what about the Second World War? There were reporters and newspapers then too, not to mention airplanes to get them around faster than this paper did. Look at the dates. Eighth of May when it actually happened in April. Two weeks later. In the 1940s, everyone had radios, and even went to watch the film clips that the reporters recorded. But nobody bothered much about what the Nazis were doing to the Jews, did they?"

Judy was silent. "They didn't really know what was happening, did they?" she finally asked.

"No. The Nazis were pretty good at manipulating the news. And hiding things. And even when things did get out, people thought they were propaganda. Or simple exaggeration. You know, 'the enemy does such horrible things,' just to get the people going. For that matter, some people even today think it's all exaggerated."

"You're right," Judy admitted. "Six million is such a mind-boggling number. It's only when you read a book about one person at a time that you're willing to believe a bit of it. Maybe that's why *The Diary of Anne Frank* is such a popular book."

"But Judy," Malka explained, "when you're part of it you know that six million is probably an underestimate. You think of the cities where you grew up, where on a Shabbos morning, the streets were filled with people going to shul, and now, there's not a Jew to be seen. It's not just individuals that died. It's whole communities."

"But people survived," Judy protested. "You said yourself that your grandmother came over from Poland after the war."

"My grandmother," Malka laughed. "My grandmother was the youngest of six children. She had aunts and uncles and cousins, all living in the vibrant community of Lemberg. I don't really know much about what happened

## Chapter Thirteen

to her. She won't talk about it, even though lately, it's starting to come out a bit. But one thing I can tell you. She's got one niece who lives in America, and two cousins in Israel. And that's it."

"How did she get to England?"

"I'm really not sure," Malka admitted. "I think she was with a friend in the DP camp after the war. You know, those were camps where they packed in all the survivors until they could find a country that was willing to let them in. And that friend had a brother in London so when she went to join him, she dragged my grandmother along with her. It made no difference to my grandmother where she went, you see. She had no home to go back to and nothing to take along."

Nothing to take along. Judy tried to imagine a person starting all over again, with absolutely nothing, besides her memories, to remind her of what she had left behind. She thought of the little brooch in her mother's jewelery box, and she suddenly realized how very precious it was to her.

"That's why my father is so happy to have been able to do this project for her," Malka continued. "Even though it's such an expense. It's the one thing she has left from her family."

"What is?"

"The *sefer Torah*. Didn't I tell you?" Malka looked surprised. "I'd started to a few times, but we kept getting onto other things. It belonged to my grandfather, I think, and he hid it during the war. From what we just read, you can understand why. And now it's been found."

Judy blinked. "Now? So many years later? How did that happen?"

"It's a very long story. My father said he'll show it to me and tell me all about it; it's coming back from the *sofer* tomorrow."

"The *sofer*?"

"That's the man who writes it and checks it and fixes the parts that have been damaged by time," Malka explained. "It was in pretty good condition though, considering, and it's supposed to be a really beautiful script. They've put it through the computer already and now it's perfect."

"Computer? What on earth do you mean?"

Malka laughed. "Quite a procedure," she explained. "There's actually a computer program nowadays that checks through the entire scroll to make sure there's not a single mistake. I don't know if you've ever seen a *sefer Torah* up close, but it's written entirely by hand. It's so easy to make a mistake and so hard for the eye to catch one."

Judy thought of the *sefer Torah* written by Reb Simcha the *Kohen*, the one laboriously scripted with quill and ink, line by line, over an entire year. And according to Malka, that was still how it was done today.

"Didn't think you'd use a computer for something as old-fashioned as a *sefer Torah*," she commented.

"It's not old-fashioned," Malka said quietly. "Just old."

Judy digested that in silence. She remembered again how easily the large volume had made the transition from the rough wooden table in the Ukraine, to the house on Kyverdale Road; how comfortably it lay on the large dining room table in Malka's house under the fluorescent lighting.

Sudden footsteps sounded on the front path outside, and the girls looked at each other in dismay.

"It really is Penny this time," Judy said ruefully, as she swept all the the papers back into a pile. "What do we do now?"

## Chapter Thirteen

"Pity, isn't it?" Malka winced. A sudden thought struck her. "I've got it, Judy. My grandmother."

"Your grandmother?"

"Yes. Don't you see? She's coming tomorrow too, to see the *sefer Torah*. She hasn't seen it yet; she was away when it arrived and my father took it straight away to the *sofer*. I'm sure my grandmother will be able to read that Yiddish. We could ask her. Do you want to come over with the letters tomorrow morning? She'll be here by ten, she said."

Judy hesitated. Sharing her find with Malka had come naturally; would it be the same with an adult? But she'd come this far and she couldn't stop here. She'd have to take all of this further, as far as she possibly could.

"Alright," she said rapidly, as she heard the sound of a key in the rusty lock. "But what do I tell Penny?"

"Tell her you finally got to work on that project of yours," Malka answered immediately. "And you're coming over to interview me as one of your natives."

"Good idea," Judy grinned. She sped upstairs with her precious armload, and slipped it back into the zippered pocket. Then she pounded downstairs to meet Penny as she opened the door.

"Oh, hi Judy. I'm sorry I was gone so long," Penny panted. She seemed to have run half the way home. "Here I am, promising your Mum I'll look after you and I'm leaving you alone after dark. Oh, hello. Sorry. Didn't realize you've got company."

Penny eyed Malka uncertainly, then seemed reassured by her pleasant smile. Judy stood tongue-tied, a sudden unaccountable awkwardness seizing her as she stood between the two girls.

"You've got reason to be worried," Malka said, covering for Judy. "She went and locked herself out. But don't worry. She spent the day with us and then Bill came over with a key."

"Oh, you left your key?! Now I feel even worse!" Penny said. She turned to Malka. "Thanks ever so much."

"My pleasure," Malka answered, easing her way past Penny towards the door. "Will I see you tomorrow, Judy? I'll make some time in the morning, if you still want my help with your project."

"I don't believe it, Judy," Penny laughed. "You mean you've actually done something constructive while I was away? Maybe I'd better do some shopping tomorrow after all and leave you to it."

Judy shrugged. "I've got to try, haven't I?" she said evasively, trying to keep her smile natural. She turned to Malka. "Alright, then, thanks so much. Can I come over in the morning?"

"Sure. I'll see you then." And with a wave of her hand, Malka was gone.

"Sorry again that I'm so late," Penny said, tossing her anorak in the corner of the kitchen. "I'd had no idea I took the key! I boarded that silly Underground in the wrong direction and ended up somewhere in Lambeth."

Judy laughed. "Some fisherman's daughter you are. Can't tell the difference between North and South! And do stop berating yourself over the key — it was my own fault, and it all worked out okay in the end."

"That's a relief." Penny plopped down on the orange crate and stretched her aching legs. "Oof!" she groaned. "Never mind the Underground. I kept getting lost wherever I went today, even with my trusty map. Guess I don't have your sense of direction."

"My sense of direction?" Judy blinked. "I'm the one who's been following you and your map all around."

"Oh, I know," Penny shrugged. "It's just that I'm usu-

## Chapter Thirteen

ally content just to muddle along as I go, and you're the one who always has a clear idea of which way you're headed."

"Do you think so? Even here in London?"

Penny stopped and contemplated the question. "No," she finally admitted, eyeing her friend gravely. "For some reason, things are different here in London."

Small homey sounds filled the silence that fell between the two tired girls; they sliced and rinsed vegetables for their salad, fried some eggs and buttered slices of bread, while the kettle hissed companionably. Still, Judy was beginning to feel like a square peg in a round hole, like she was trying to sit in a place that was gradually growing tighter.

She wondered if it were true; had she always known where she was heading? Suddenly, everything seemed to be shifting around her. She felt like she had spent all her life building a sand castle down by the beach and now she was watching the tide come in, covering it all and washing it out to sea. She'd have to start again, she knew, only this time she'd build something a bit more solid, and a bit higher up the bank, where the waters couldn't reach it.

Judy sat by the table, idly picking at the congealed egg on her plate. She wasn't really hungry; she'd eaten more just this one afternoon than all of these past few days put together. When Penny stretched and yawned again, she welcomed the suggestion for an early night. She was looking forward to tomorrow. But first she needed a good night's sleep to digest today.

## Chapter Fourteen

Judy was surprised to find that she had actually slept a peaceful, dreamless night. After she'd gone to bed, the packet had silently nagged at her through her sleeping bag as she lay there in her usual position; Penny fast asleep while Judy, wide awake, shifted uneasily from side to side. She had finally crept out to the landing again with the precious papers in her hand and settled herself on the step.

This time, she didn't bother with the letters; she was content to leave them to Malka's grandmother. Instead, she went for the English newspapers, determined to plow through them from beginning to end. The print was small enough to fill page after page with facts and figures; numbers that stunned her as she read. There were lists of towns destroyed by the pillagers, along with the names of the dead and injured. Appeals by organizations in London that had banded together to help the survivors; some with food and clothing, some with medicines and hospital care. Still others arranged passports and visas, letters of recommendation, and finally, the steamship tickets that spelled ultimate salvation from the pogroms of Russia: emigration. England, America, wherever. As long as it was many miles away from Odessa and the shouts of the mobs.

After Judy had finally finished reading, she had collapsed into her sleeping bag, but she was afraid to close her eyes. Just reading the papers had been a nightmare; she hoped there wasn't another to follow. But the next thing she knew, the smell of coffee was curling up the steps, rousing her from a quiet slumber.

When she came downstairs, Penny had her nose in an advertising sheet that had come through the door. "Not much left of the Sunday trading laws," she commented as Judy poured herself a drink. "Says here that the Shopping City is open today and there are some good sales. You in the mood or are you really serious about working on your project?"

Judy took a long sip of the hot tea. "I think I'll stick to my project," she said casually. "Do you mind going out on your own?"

"No. I guess not." Penny eyed her carefully. "Sure you're sure?"

"Sure."

Malka's grandmother was just as Judy had imagined. Soft and cushiony with smiling blue-grey eyes. A certain sad wisdom lurked behind them though, as if keeping company with the thoughts and memories she was hiding behind her smile. Judy wondered suddenly if it was fair to show her the articles that she had read the night before. As she had sat on the landing, immersed in the fine English print, she had felt as if a film projector had been activated in her brain, replaying the terrible scenes she had seen that Friday night, in the doorway of the front room on Kyverdale Road. She had relived the fear Yehudis had felt as she gazed down on her sleeping child, as she listened to the shouts of the mob, and watched her front door being slowly pushed open. Yet, no matter

## Chapter Fourteen

how realistic that had been, it was still all a dream. How then would Mrs. Meyer feel, reading the detailed print on the newspaper sheet? Her experiences had been real and firsthand. Judy did not wish to hurt her by summoning up such frightening memories. She only wanted to find more pieces for her fragmented puzzle.

The fragrant kitchen was as warm as the welcome they gave her, yet Judy stood awkwardly in the doorway, watching Malka's mother remove a steaming tray of biscuits from the hot oven.

"So this is Judy," Mrs. Meyer smiled, as Malka introduced her. "Malka was just telling me about you. She says that you have something you would like me to read."

"If it wouldn't be too much trouble," Judy answered, suddenly shy. "Do you have the time for it?"

"Until Malka's father returns, definitely," Mrs. Meyer answered. "Then you will have to excuse me for a while. I will want to hear what he has to tell us. Malka has told you about our excitement?"

Judy nodded.

"But now I have time." She broke off suddenly, remembering something she'd forgotten. "The mantle." She turned to her daughter. "Did it come in time?"

Mrs. Fishman nodded reassuringly. "They delivered it late last night and Mendel took it with him to the *sofer*. It's not the same as the one you've described, of course, but still, it's lovely. You'll be happy when you see it."

Mrs. Meyer nodded her satisfaction and turned back to Judy. "Come, sit down." She patted the kitchen chair beside her invitingly. "Why don't you show me what you have."

Malka's mother smiled at her encouragingly as Judy gently pulled out the bundle and spread it out on the kitchen table.

"There are letters and newspaper clippings," Judy explained. "Mostly in Yiddish, Malka says. I've read the ones in English and I imagine that the Yiddish ones are more of the same."

She winced inwardly as Mrs. Meyer reached for the newspaper first. "It's basically the letters I'm really interested in," she said hastily. "The articles are pretty awful."

Malka's grandmother eyed her thoughtfully for a moment and fingered the pile of newspaper clippings. Then she adjusted her glasses and began to read to herself.

"You're right, Judy," she said quietly, after a few moments. "Russia, 1903, *was* pretty awful." She picked up the small square pamphlets. "*Di Kishinev Hariga*," she read. "Published by the Bund in 1903. *Pogromen Blatt*. Also by the Bund. They used them in their appeals for money. *Thousands demonstrate in New York*," she continued.

"So people did protest," Malka commented.

"So it seems," Mrs. Meyer agreed. "But it probably didn't help much."

She leafed through the remaining pile. "Another appeal for money. This one seems to be an argument for sending a hospital ship to Odessa. I doubt if that ever got anywhere." She smiled. "And here we have Baron Hirsch's grand scheme for making a Jewish colony on his land in Argentina. It sounds very good, doesn't it?"

"Argentina?" Judy gaped. "Anything come of it?"

"Nothing much. Eventually everything came to a halt with the First World War. That misery drowned everything. Even the progroms."

She gently replaced the newspaper onto the table and smiled at Judy. "Shall we try one of the letters?" she said, deliberately matter-of-fact.

## Chapter Fourteen

Judy handed her the pile of envelopes and watched her carefully open the one at the top. "Beautiful handwriting," she commented as she began to read. "Now this one is dated 5641. What is that number we always take away?"

"3760," Malka said quietly. "Let's see, that makes it 1881."

"What's that?" Judy was bewildered. "I don't understand."

"We count from the year the world was created," Malka explained, ignoring Judy's incredulous look. "A difference of 3760 years. Add that number to any English date and you'll have the Hebrew one. Only we write it in Hebrew lettering, not numbers. I'll explain it to you another time," she added quickly. "We've gotten the date now. Let's hear the rest."

The kitchen was quiet as they watched Mrs. Meyer slowly decipher the page, her eyes moving down the paper, line by line. When she finished, she stared quietly ahead of her for a moment, then looked down at the paper before her, as if trying to see if there was more between the lines.

She looked at the eager faces before her. "I'm not a very good interpreter," she finally said. "And it's not just a matter of understanding the handwriting. This letter is written very, very carefully, by someone who knows that with one wrong word, it wouldn't get past the censor. It seems to refer to things that only the people for whom it was meant would understand. Listen and see what you make of this." She read:

> To my very dear Yehudis and Leibel,
>
> I hope that all is well with you and little Chaya'le and that you have settled down nicely in your new home. I trust that it is not too far from your old home and

163

friends, in spirit as well. Here in Kiev all is as well as it can possibly be. The big is not always better than the small. Blessed are those whose portion has taken them far.

Your loving father who misses you<br>and blesses you with peace

There was silence in the kitchen as she finished.

"Is that it?" Judy asked quietly.

"I'm afraid so," Mrs. Meyer said, looking down again at the yellowing paper. "I am sorry to disappoint you."

"I can't really make heads or tails of it, Judy," Malka said, wrinkling her nose in perplexity. "Can you?"

Judy was silent, feverishly trying to think of something to say. The letter was very clear to her; she understood it as well as she would have, had it been written out in English, ten pages long. She could hear the worry in Reb Simcha's voice as it sounded across the miles. *You have moved away from the East End, and I'm glad. But how far away from the shul is it? In which direction have you moved?*

Malka's voice sounded plaintively in the silent kitchen. "*The big is not always better than the small!* What on earth does he mean?"

The cryptic remark made too much sense to Judy; she could feel the pain as it knifed through her. The family had run to Kiev from the little Ukrainian village. There's safety in numbers, they'd thought. But Reb Simcha had been right in urging Yehudis to go further. Pogroms had swept Kiev as well, soon after they'd arrived there; the first round of riots had broken out when the Czar was assassinated. Czar Alexander II. Judy knew because she had read about it last night, in that paper so aptly entitled, "Darkest Russia." She shivered. *Blessed are those whose portion has taken them far.*

## Chapter Fourteen

Judy felt her face grow hot under the curious gaze of the others in the kitchen. Say something quick, she silently prodded herself. "Do you think," she finally brought out, "do you think that he's trying to tell them that they're lucky they got away from where he is? My great-uncle Martin may have told..."

The sound of the key in the front door saved her, just in time; she had no idea how to finish her sentence.

Mrs. Meyer scraped her chair back from the table, her eyes taking a deeper hue as an eager smile lit her face. "Is that Mendel?"

Malka dashed out into the hallway as a warm hello sounded from the open door. "He's here!"

The excitement in her voice flowed like an electric current through the kitchen, lighting the faces of the two older women as they rushed to join her in the dining room. Judy felt somewhat out of place, and didn't know whether to follow. She could hear a happy murmur as they greeted Rabbi Fishman and then she heard the sound of something heavy being carefully laid on the table. Then silence. She took a tentative step towards the doorway, and hesitated.

"Judy?" Malka's sudden call made her jump. "You can come in too, you know."

Judy could feel the emotions that played in the room as she entered. There was a charged atmosphere that she could almost touch and she stood quietly near the doorway, not wanting to intrude.

Mrs. Fishman stood near the dining room table, her arm around her mother's shoulder.

"I'm sure it was the same Yossel," Mrs. Meyer finally said, breaking the silence. Her voice sounded as if it were coming from a very long distance. "Yossel the blacksmith. My father managed to tell him where he had hidden it,

165

before they took him away." She took a deep breath. "Yossel had muscles of steel. The Nazis needed him. They kept him for what he was worth, probably till the end. I wouldn't know for sure. I was gone before then." She looked about her with unseeing eyes. "But he wouldn't be alive by now anyway, would he, even if he did outlive the Nazis. I wonder if it was his son who brought it out of the box."

"Did this Yossel have a son?" Rabbi Fishman's voice was deep with emotion.

She shook her head in frustration. "I don't know. He didn't live near us, more towards the end of the town, and I never knew his family. Yossel, we called him. That's all. But it *must* be the same person."

Judy watched her reach out and touch what lay before her on the table. "So beautiful," she sighed.

The clock ticked loudly in the quiet room as Malka turned around and gestured to Judy. "Want to see?" she mouthed.

Judy stepped forward hesitantly, almost on tiptoe, coming around the corner of the table, where no one would block her view. The new velvet mantle *was* beautiful, with gold embroidery delicately etched onto the rich blue fabric. But Judy barely noticed it. Her eyes grew wide and they glazed with a sudden film of tears as she stared at the *atzei chayim* that reached out towards her from under their velvet cover. There was no mistaking the thick and rounded shafts, beautifully carved, then distinctively twisted at the end, like pointed flames above a candle.

Judy reached out a hesitant finger and touched the sculpted swirls in the warm golden wood. It can't be, she thought in sudden confusion. Or was she back in her dream that she'd struggled so hard to get out of? But the

## Chapter Fourteen

fluorescent fixture hung starkly from the ceiling, lighting up the scene with a glaring whiteness that allowed no mistake. She looked up to see Malka eyeing her curiously and she coughed to cover the lump in her throat. "Do they all look like this?" she finally trusted herself to ask. "I mean the poles, or whatever you call them. Are they all pointed and carved like this?"

"Actually not," Rabbi Fishman replied. "Most of them have smooth, rounded handles. That's what makes this *sefer Torah* so very distinctive. The *atzei chayim* are a work of art." He turned to Malka's grandmother. "You had described them very well. I knew this was the *sefer Torah*, as soon as my cousin, Reb Shmuel, brought it into the room."

"Reb Shmuel?" Judy asked in confusion. "I thought he lives in Lvov. How did he get it? Wasn't the *sefer Torah* hidden in Poland?"

"The *sefer Torah* was hidden in Poland, Judy," Rabbi Fishman replied. "In the city of Lemberg, where my mother-in-law lived. After the war, Lemberg was taken by the Russians," he calmly continued. "They call it Lvov. It's a fair sized city somewhere in the Ukraine."

CHAPTER FIFTEEN

The Ukraine. The words stood out from the jumble of sounds around her in the same way that the *atzei chayim* were superimposed on the haze that suddenly covered the room. As Judy stared at them in fascination, the room receded into a blur. She felt as if she was looking at a frame of trick photography, where the subject is centered in sure stark detail, and all the rest of the scene is whitewashed into the background. As if from some remote broadcast, she could hear Rabbi Fishman's voice in the distance.

"He must be the blacksmith's son," he was saying. "A big broad fellow with an honest face and a huge grin that makes everyone smile with him. Not that he has much to smile about. No family that I know of. He lives in one of those small houses at the end of the town. The poor section. It makes sense, now that we think of it. They've never gotten around to knocking down the old houses to build those huge blocks of flats. In that section of town, it's still the same as it was before the war. At least, that's what I was told; I never got there myself. And somewhere, in one of the walls, they'd hidden the *sefer Torah*."

"In the wall?"

"In the wall. He said his father had returned to Lemberg after the war. No one called it Lemberg anymore; that was what the Austrians had called it, long ago. Once they had gone, only the Jews called it Lemberg, but the postal address had always been Lvov and that's what it's called today. Since the war, there were no longer any Jews there to speak of who would call it by any other name. A few Jews had come straggling back, for lack of anywhere else to go. Yossel had returned to his house at the outskirts of the city, which somehow still remained standing. Miraculously, his wife had come back too and a few years later their son Sasha was born.

"During those first few months after the war had ended, the city center was a heap of ruins and rubble. Giant cranes would soon come to level it all and build the communist answer to housing problems — giant boxes filled with flats, like dozens of eggs in a tray. The wheels of the Soviet bureaucracy would start turning as well, and Yossel was well aware of what would follow. The terror of Stalin had abated somewhat during the war years, but as he'd move to consolidate power over the newly annexed areas, the terror would build to unbearable peaks. For now, Yossel knew that his movements were relatively unhindered and, according to Sasha, that was when he searched the old quarter for the house of Reb Berisch.

"It wasn't easy. He combed the pockmarked pavements for signs of where the old houses had stood. Some of them were empty shells and some of them simply craters in the ground. But he found the house, more or less intact. The upper floor was gone, the roof caved in and the rooms emptied of anything that could be carried away. But the front room was there, blocked by mounds of rubble, and he found the *sefer Torah*, in the exact place that Reb Berisch had told him he'd hidden it away.

"He carried it through the streets, holding the old

## Chapter Fifteen

wooden crate casually under his arm, as if it were empty. He bunched some sticks of broken chair slats into his second massive fist, to complete the illusion of the typical resident, carrying home kindling for his fire. Once he was safely home, he hollowed out a place for the *sefer Torah*, behind the wall of his front room. There it stayed in silent safety, through the terror of Stalin and the heavy hand of Khrushchev and the ones who followed. There was no use for it anyway; the last shul left in Lvov, they turned into a youth club.

"Only Yossel's wife knew what lay behind the wall," Rabbi Fishman continued. "And his son. Sasha told me how his father had shown him the hiding place, and he smiled as he remembered that day, happy that his father had trusted him with the secret. Not many fathers in Russia could do that. They would be risking a trip to Siberia.

"It was only a few weeks ago that Sasha decided to share the secret. He felt that it was finally safe enough, and he brought it to Reb Shmuel." Rabbi Fishman turned to his mother-in-law. "And only the week before, Reb Shmuel had received your letter."

Mrs. Meyer nodded in wonder. "My letter. Do you know how long it took me until I actually sat down to write it? I never thought that letter would be of much use," she said. "What could I find already in the Russian files that the Americans didn't have? But everyone drove me crazy. The Russians liberated so many camps, they told me. They have more Nazi files that no one has ever seen, and now that the Communists are gone, you can write and ask. What should I ask? How they were killed? When they were killed? If anyone survived, I would know by now. But I wrote. I asked your cousin Shmuel for the address and I asked him too: You live in Lemberg now.

171

Is there anyone there from the family Chayutin? 'No,' he said. 'But here is the government address that you asked for. Write to them and see what they say.' I still haven't heard anything from them, and probably never will. And yet," she smiled suddenly, "a living *sefer Torah* is also a survivor."

"Imagine how Reb Shmuel felt," her son-in-law said gently. "One week you write him about your family. Chayutin. Not a very common name. And the very next Monday, in walks this tall smiling stranger with a large wooden crate. 'Rabbi,' he says. 'I think the time has come for me to show this to you.' Imagine. A *sefer Torah* in the heart of Lvov. Such a beautiful scroll, with its unusual *atzei chayim*. Shmuel told me how he opened it. The beautiful script looked perfect, but as he unrolled it slightly, he saw that some of the ink had worked loose. A pity, he thought. Still, their newly formed minyan had a good *sefer Torah* that had been donated by his friends back in New York; he didn't really need this *sefer Torah*. It just would have been wonderful to put it back into its rightful place; in an *aron kodesh* in a shul, instead of a hiding place behind a wall. He carefully rolled it up again, and as he did so, the writing on the wood caught his eye and he couldn't believe it. *Chayutin*. He picked up the phone and he called me."

Malka's grandmother touched the wooden points gently, her finger tracing a path through the intricate carving. "You can't see the name when the mantle is on," she commented. "But we always knew it was there. We didn't keep the *sefer Torah* at home, you understand," she explained. "It was kept in the *aron kodesh*, in the shul where my father *davened*, not far from where we lived, for the minyan to use. And on Simchas Torah we loved to watch the men dance by, holding it in turn. There were

## Chapter Fifteen

many *sifrei Torah* in our shul, but we knew that the one with the beautiful handles was ours."

Malka's father gently lifted the hem of the mantle, raising it carefully until they could see the edge of the parchment. Now the rounded sphere of wood beneath the handles was visible; it topped the roll of parchment like a lid to keep it safe. Within the outer rim of the sphere, the center dipped and its surface was lighter, as if sanded down to almost parchment color; a perfect base for the lettering printed in a circular path, round the pointed handle. The letters had been engraved into the wood and then filled with ink, their carved-out niche protecting the words from fading over the years.

Judy edged forward as Rabbi Fishman's finger traced the letters, reading each word as he touched it. *Simcha ben Dov Ber Ha-Kohen Chayutin.*

"Chayutin." Malka's mother gently repeated into the silence. What is a last name after all? Judy wondered. "Chayutin" meant nothing to her, any more than the name "Schumacher" had. After all, most last names were simply something bestowed on a citizen by some long-ago registrar. It was only the first name that Judy heard, goose bumps prickling her skin as it sounded through the room. Simcha. Reb Simcha the *Kohen*. She remembered the gentle flow of his beard as he sat near the table with his daughter; the melodious tones of his voice as he chanted the blessing for peace. *V'yasem l'cha shalom.* The words on the sphere seemed to swirl around in their circular path to the tune of the blessing that rang through her thoughts. It was strange how at that moment, each ear in the room was attuned to it own particular song.

"Dov Ber Ha-Kohen," Malka's grandmother said quietly. "Some long-ago grandfather, but that was my father's name. Everyone knew him as Berisch."

She sighed softly, remembering. "When the first rumbles of war reached Lemberg, my father took the *sefer Torah* home. No one knew who would reach us first; the Germans or the Russians, and he trusted neither of them. Behind the tall wardrobe in our salon, there was a built-in cupboard that we never used. You couldn't even see the door; the wardrobe was huge and heavy. My father placed the *sefer Torah* in a crate and put it up on the very top shelf at the back. We didn't even know about it. He only told us later, when they set up the ghetto. I suppose he hoped that someone would come back in the end and get it. He couldn't have known how bad it would get, or how desperate we would be to get away, when it would all be finally over. I had my chance to reach London. Coming back to Lvov would have been asking for trouble. The Russians would never have let me leave again."

Her hands moved restlessly, fingering the golden fringe of the mantle. "I saw him that morning, deep in conversation with Yossel. I'm sure he told him then about the *sefer Torah*. I remember him telling my brother as he walked into the house, 'I told Yossel.' And somehow, I thought he meant the *sefer Torah*. But I never knew for sure. I never saw either of them after that. I was at the factory when the first transport went." She swallowed. "To Belzec."

They sat in silence, not daring to interrupt the very first words she had ever shared with them about the war. It was a warm silence that listened, sharing the sorrow, its lack of words a comfort all its own. Her eyes gazed inwards, towards those hidden thoughts and memories, and then she roused herself again, her hand still fingering the mantel fringe.

"One from a family, two from a town. Handpicked by Heaven, who should survive. That's what we see when we

## Chapter Fifteen

look at each person separately, and count each survivor, one by one. It's only when we look at *Klal Yisrael*, the Jewish people as one, that we realize that Hashem has never forsaken us. Sick and broken, but alive, and ready to rebuild. Go on to other places and start again." She paused. "And the *sefer Torah* goes along."

"That is the way it has been, every since the *Beis Ha-mikdash* was destroyed." Rabbi Fishman said quietly. "We go from place to place, sometimes by choice, and sometimes by force. And each time it's a reminder to beg Hashem, please, when will we finally be allowed to come home?

"How did Jews get to Russia in the first place?" he continued. "Most of them were refugees from decrees and expulsions in Germany, where they'd lived since Roman times. Over the years, they went on to Poland, Lithuania and finally up to Russia. The Georgian Jews were there even earlier. They moved there from Bavel, after the first *Beis Ha-mikdash*, and never went back. If you look at the map you can see that Georgia is just beyond Iraq. The Gemara even tells us how Rabbi Akiva journeyed to the mountains of Ararat to collect money for *tzedakah*. That's right near Georgia. And that's how the people in those distant communities kept up with *Klal Yisrael*. Think of it," he smiled. "They would never have learned Mishnah or Gemara, if there were no such thing as a *meshulach!*"

Mrs. Meyer smiled faintly. "And how many journeys has this particular *sefer Torah* taken?" she wondered aloud. "This long-ago grandfather, Simcha ben Dov Ber Ha-Kohen. Where did he live? What did he experience? How can we ever know? Yet we are what we are today, because of what he was then." She paused.

"And the *sefer Torah* is here with us again."

"It's not very usual to have a name on a *sefer Torah*,"

175

Rabbi Fishman commented. "I've seen it only one or two times before. And once, it was written in faint ink on the actual parchment, along the very end of the scroll where it's sewn to the wood."

"A pity there is no date," he continued. "When you get to know a little bit, you are always hungry for more."

Judy sat still at the table, in wondering, frustrated silence. She had learned so much from this quiet conversation, yet there was so much that she could add, if only she could tell them. And there was so much more they could tell her if they knew what she knew.

"*Knew*." There was that word again. But didn't she mean, "*thought* she knew"? What was real and what was imagined? How could she know if she indeed possessed the secrets of her ancestors? How much had she actually heard at one time or another from Uncle Martin? Did she dare to tell these people about her dreams?

Soon, she told herself. Very soon she would reveal everything, even if it made her appear foolish. There was too much evidence piling up for her "dreams" to have been anything but the truth. It had to be. Judy knew that somewhere, somehow, *she belonged to this family.*

## Chapter Sixteen

No one had seen Mrs. Fishman quietly leave the room; now she entered, bearing a tray with hot tea and biscuits, and the fragrant cloud that preceded her gently lightened the mood. The family sat together in silence, sipping the hot tea slowly, as if in silent consent, knowing that when the cups were empty this little interlude in their busy schedules would end. Judy took a bite, chewing reflectively as the taste of hot ginger flooded her mouth. She caught Malka's eye and they smiled companionably.

"Will you have time to read some more of Judy's letters?" Malka asked her grandmother, as she reached for another biscuit.

"I don't mind," she smiled. "We've been making a lot of journeys into the past today. We may as well continue."

"What's this about letters?" Rabbi Fishman asked, as Judy went to the kitchen to fetch them.

"The letters I told you about, late last night," Malka reminded him. "The ones that Bill found up in the attic next door. I think they're all in Yiddish, and Bubbe said she'll try to read them for us."

They settled themselves quietly back in their chairs as Mrs. Meyer adjusted her glasses for a second time that morning. She shuffled through the pile of envelopes, carefully choosing the ones with the handwriting she'd read earlier. There were only three of them; the rest she put aside.

"Now let's see," she calculated quickly in her mind. "This one would be dated 1886. Nisan 1886."

> My very dear Yehudis and Leibel,
>
> I hope that you are very well both in body and in spirit. Time passes so quickly and your little Chaya'le has already reached the age of bas mitzvah. May she truly be a daughter who does many mitzvos, even in the wide world of London. May she walk in the ways of her grandmother *z"l*, who lived only for Torah and mitzvos.
>
> Yehudis, your mother has gone to a better world than the one we live in, where all her mitzvos and good deeds have been waiting to greet her. During all the days of her long illness, she never wanted to be a burden on anyone, taking care to call me only when she absolutely needed something, so as not to disturb my learning. Her last thoughts were of you and your family, happy that you are far from the many troubles.
>
> We await *Mashiach* to speedily come in our days and bring an end to all sorrow. May the peace that you have found in London bring you only blessing.
>
> Your loving father

There was silence in the kitchen as Mrs. Meyer gently refolded the paper and inserted it into the envelope. She didn't ask if she should continue; she simply picked up the next one and, taking out the yellowing sheet, she looked at the date and began.

Tamuz 1888

> My very dear Yehudis and Leibel,

## Chapter Sixteen

> I hope all is well with you in London. We think of you always and hope that you are not worrying about us too much. A happy event in a family pushes away much of the sorrow. Last week was the wedding of Chananya's youngest son, Nachum Pesach, and all the family gathered for the simchah. Leibel, your sister Mirel has found that feathers can fly across the sea. May we find peace wherever we go.
>
> Your loving father

"Across the sea," Mrs. Fishman whispered. "They must have emigrated to America like so many others. But why feathers?"

Judy sat still, remembering the three little girls who had sorted the feathers for their mother to sell. There was no way she could know if all of them had left the country safely and arrived at the other shore. But one thing she *did* know was that Yehudis hated feathers. The cryptic reference in the letter made her wonder.

Mrs. Meyer's voice broke the silence as she unfolded the next letter. "The writing is still the same, but slightly shaky," she commented as she looked carefully at the page. "Look. Some of the lines at the bottom are running into each other, as if they were written by night, in the dark. Or do you think...?" She checked the date. "It's more than a year later. Adar 1889. And that's the last one in this handwriting." She began to read:

> My very dear Yehudis and Leibel,
>
> It is hard for me to write; my eyesight is not very good. The years of fine writing have left their mark. Chaim Pinchas sends his sons in to learn a bit with me and that revives me each day. I think of you so often, and hope to hear only good, from near and from far. We hope for the days when *Mashiach* will come and unite

those who have wandered to the four distant corners of the earth. May the threefold blessing follow you always.

Your loving father

Rabbi Fishman cleared his throat in the long silence that followed. "Do you recognize any of these names?" he asked, turning to Judy.

"Some of them," Judy said carefully, choosing each word as she spoke. "Yehudis was the grandmother who originally came to the house next door. My great-uncle told me about her when he gave me a brooch which belonged to her. Her name is inscribed on it: Yehudis."

She hesitated. "I'm actually named after her. Judy is short for Judith."

Malka's father raised an eyebrow. "Your mother couldn't have known her."

Judy shook her head. "No, of course not. But my Uncle Martin says she still lived here when he was very small. It was Granny Vi whom my mother knew," she explained. "My mother's great-grandmother. It seems she made my mother promise she'd give her daughter that name. And my mother remembered that promise, even though she was barely twelve at the time."

"Granny Vi," Rabbi Fishman said thoughtfully. "That would be Vivian, wouldn't it?"

"I suppose so."

"You do know your French, I'm sure," he smiled. "*Vive* for life. But do you know your Hebrew?" He nodded and smiled again. "Your Granny Vi must have been the little Chaya'le."

Judy nodded obediently, trying to look surprised. "It makes sense," she finally said. "And Leibel must be her father."

## Chapter Sixteen

Mrs. Meyer eyed her carefully, then looked down at the letter in her hand. "The threefold blessing," she said quietly. "Does that mean anything to you?"

Rabbi Fishman stopped short. "I hadn't noticed that," he admitted. "The threefold blessing of a *kohen*. I wonder why he should choose those words."

"Judy," Malka leaned forward in excitement. "The hands!"

"What hands?" Mrs. Fishman turned to her daughter.

Judy took a deep breath. "The brooch that I got is an old-fashioned bar pin," she explained. "The letters of the name *Yehudis* are swirled across, and on top there are two hands engraved in a strange position. With the two thumbs together." She paused. "Uncle Martin said it's the blessing of a *kohen*."

"The threefold blessing," Mrs. Meyer repeated. "The blessing of peace. He mentions it again and again in his letters, doesn't he? Her father must have been a *kohen*." She smiled pleasantly. "So we've found some useful information in your letters, Judy. Now you know a bit more about where you come from and who your grandfather was."

*If only you knew*, Judy screamed silently as she stared at the pile of envelopes. *There is so much more I could tell you, that you've missed, but I can't. Didn't you read what he says about the tiny print that weakened his eyes; the years he spent writing, things like your* sefer Torah? *And Chananya. He created your beautiful* atzei chayim. She thought feverishly. *But I don't know who the others are. Who could they be? Where do they all fit in?*

She gathered up the remaining letters, suddenly impatient, then forced herself to remain calm. It was all so unbearably frustrating. "Do you think you have time for these?" she asked.

"Time?" Malka's grandmother smiled as the others sat back in their chairs, intent on continuing. "For these letters, Judy, all the time in the world." She withdrew the letter at the top and squinted down at the writing. "I'm afraid these will be a little more difficult. The other letters were beautifully written, each letter perfectly formed. But look at *this* script."

Judy had to smile. Loops and flourishes filled the page, as ornamental as the intricate carving on the *atzei chayim.*

"Iyar 1890," Mrs. Meyer began.

To my very dear sister and brother-in-law,

> I am sure you have been worried all this long time that you have received no news from us. For some time, I did not mail the last letter of our father, for I knew you would worry when you saw how it was written. But then, he suffered with his eyesight for many years, as you surely must remember. Even in your time, he no longer wrote. In the end, I sent you the letter, and now I must admit that I sent it when he was no longer with us, so that you would have these last words from him for you to read and treasure. I know how it pains you to read this, but remember, Yehudis, he has gone to join our mother in a world that is better than this one, and all his Torah will stand by him forever.
>
> May we only hear good news from each other. With the blessing of peace, as our father always would say.
>
> Your brother,<br>Chananya

Mrs. Meyer flipped through the remaining envelopes, as the family sat silently, waiting. "Just two more, Judy," she said. "The others are appeal letters, along with receipts, from the Russo-Jewish Committee, based here in

## Chapter Sixteen

London. I'm sure you noticed that."

Judy nodded. She found herself sitting at the very edge of her chair as Mrs. Meyer opened the next envelope and, dropping it onto her lap, she began to read.

Tamuz 1895

> To my very dear sister and brother-in-law,
>
> I was so very glad to hear from you and receive your beautiful invitation for your Chaya'le's wedding. How I wish we could join together for our simchas. We danced for you here from afar. I am glad that you are happy with your *mechutanim*. They sound like very fine people. I hope you are happy with your son-in-law too. If the father is a *talmid chacham*, perhaps the son will also be, one day.
>
> Wishing you only mazel and joy,<br>Your brother,<br>Chananya

"And there seems to be a postscript," Mrs. Meyer said, continuing.

> Our Chaim Pinchas married off his second daughter, Itta Sheindel, last week to a very fine boy; some sort of cousin from his wife's family in Lemberg. I'm afraid it's a bit complicated to explain. Like our mother used to say: *ferd, fuss, podkiva, tshvock's an einikel.*"

Malka's grandmother broke off with a laugh. "My mother always said that too, when we tried to trace some relative." She looked at Judy and tried to explain. "It sounds much better in Yiddish so what can I tell you? It goes something like this: If someone is distantly related, you say he's the horse's, foot's, shoe's, nail's grandson!"

She laughed to herself again, and then her smile

seemed to freeze suddenly on her face, and slowly melt into a frown of intent concentration as she absorbed all at once what she'd read. "Chaim Pinchas," she whispered. "Itta Sheindel. Who *are* these people?"

She looked down at the letter and then lifted the envelope from her lap, turning it over carefully in her hand. Judy held her breath. She could see the scrawl on the triangular fold of the envelope; the one return address that she'd never been able to read. She leaned forward for a closer look, and the illegible scrawl sprang suddenly to life as Malka's grandmother read the name aloud, her voice vibrating like the strings of a violin.

"*Chayutin!*"

A sharp hiss sounded in the room as four breaths were drawn in sharply, simultaneously. Judy looked around at their faces gone suddenly pale and tried to appropriately arrange her facial features. She felt like she had entered her house and everyone shouted, "Surprise," but she'd known all along about the party and now she had to pretend that she didn't. Yet the smile that lit her face mirrored the gladness that flooded her senses. It felt like years had elapsed since she'd seen the *sefer Torah* on the dining room table, but it was only about an hour since she'd discovered that she belonged to this family. And now they knew it too.

A heavy silence fell in the kitchen, each mouth opening and closing again, as they searched for the words that expressed what they wanted to say. Even Rabbi Fishman seemed at a loss; his mouth worked soundlessly as he stared at the envelope in his mother-in-law's hand.

"Chaim Pinchas," Mrs. Meyer whispered, looking up at her family in wonder. "My grandfather. That was how my father was called up each Shabbos in Shul, 'Dov Ber ben Chaim Pinchas ha-Kohen.' And my Tanta Itta." She

## Chapter Sixteen

shook her head, as if arousing herself from a trance and reached for the remaining letter.

"Iyar 1903," she read.

To my dear sister and brother-in-law,

> I hope you are all well, and that you receive this letter. I see from your words that my others have not gotten through. I am sure there are newspapers in London. The *korbanos* have been dreadful. May we merit to bring the true *korbanos* in the *Beis Ha-mikdash*, rebuilt speedily in our days.
>
> Here in Kiev it is only the words that are frightening as yet. They spread on the wings of rumor and no one knows what to do. Yet, there are more shops that are closing for Shabbos as people begin to realize why all this befalls us.
>
> Nachum Pesach and his family remain here with me but his brothers have gone to sea. My oldest son, Chaim Pinchas, does not like the desert across the water, so he has gone to join his wife's family, where his three married daughters already live. His children have been the closest to me all the years and I will miss them; most of all my youngest grandson, the little Berisch. I have sent the *sefer Torah* with them, away from the fires.
>
> Your brother,
> Chananya

The ticking of the clock on the wall sounded to Judy like the clicking of tiny puzzle pieces falling into place.

"Families," Rabbi Fishman was the first to break the stillness with a single word. He reached out a finger in wonder and touched the *sefer Torah* that lay before them on the table. "How families have been tossed around from place to place, separated by miles of land and sea. Decades later they end up in the house next door, like the *sefer Torah* and the letters that tell us how far it has traveled."

He mused at the marvel of it all for a few moments, in the continuing silence of the room that the others could not yet break, then he gave a sudden smile.

"Can you understand now," he said, turning to Judy, "how all Jews feel themselves to be brothers? Wherever I travel, if I see a mezuzah, I know I've got a relative there to help me. We're part of one family, even though that family has been flung around to every spot on the globe."

"I guess it makes sense," Judy said in a small voice. "I mean I've got two parents, four grandparents, and eight great-grandparents. If you go back a few generations, you'll get hundreds of people related to me and hundreds of people related to you, even though there were fewer people in the world then than there are today. It must be that somewhere we go back to the very same people."

"We do go back to the very same people," Rabbi Fishman said. "As soon as we read that your grandfather was a *kohen* and our grandfather was a *kohen*, we knew that thousands of years ago, we went back to the very first *kohen*. But as you said so well, we don't have to go back that far. It's only a few short decades back to Simcha ben Dov Ber Ha-Kohen." He paused. "'Even in your time, he no longer wrote,'" he quoted. "We all missed that as we read, didn't we? The small fine print. Yehudis must have still been very young when the *sefer Torah* was written. We have no date on our *atzei chayim*, but we can see from these precious letters, that even in 1903, the *sefer Torah* was old, when he sent it to Lemberg, away from the fires they knew would come to Kiev."

He turned to Judy. "Do you know what the words *siyata d'Shemaya* mean?"

She shook her head.

## Chapter Sixteen

"It literally means *help from Heaven*," he explained. "Hashem helps everyone, with food and water and air to breathe. But it's that extra help we pray for and hope to deserve. Reb Simcha had tremendous *siyata d'Shemaya*." He paused. "Just this morning, I brought the *sefer Torah* home from the *sofer*. We'd had it checked by computer, you know. It's a wonderful thing, that computer," he mused. "It finds mistakes that the ordinary eye would miss, and unfortunately, in our generation there are plenty of errors. But do you know how unusual it is to find a mistake in a *sefer Torah* from long ago? I guess they didn't need this new invention long ago," he commented. He pointed to the scroll on the table. "In this *sefer Torah* of thousands of letters, there was not a single mistake in all of it. Of course, over time some of the ink had chipped off in places and several of the panels of parchment needed restitution, but as for actual mistakes, there was not even one. That is what *siyata d'Shemaya* means. We do our best and Hashem will guide our hands to succeed. And the purer the intention, the greater the help from above."

"You can see the *siyata d'Shemaya* that Reb Simcha earned," Malka's grandmother added softly. "Today Hashem has guided his family, so that two who've gone missing have been found in one day."

Judy remembered the chain of events that had led up to this wonderful morning on Kyverdale Road. The brooch, her conversation with her uncle, and most of all, her dreams, and she understood.

Mrs. Meyer patted the envelopes lovingly into a pile. "Do you realize what you've done for us, Judy, by sharing this with us? The name on our *sefer Torah* is now a person. One very much beloved by all of us." Her smile included Judy, warming her in its glow.

"What will you do now, Judy?" Mrs. Fishman's voice

was gentle. "Will you share this with anyone else?"

"You mean, my parents?" Judy asked hesitantly. She remembered her mother's defensive posture as she spoke to Uncle Martin, that cold winter morning. Then she smiled. "They're cousins, you know, my Mum and my Dad. They'll both be interested, I think." But she knew what Malka's mother meant. Would their interest be of the practical, what-do-we-do-about-all-this-now kind, or would they be like archaeologists, objectively digging up their past, finding items as worthless as the old silver coins in the cigar box?

"I'm going to have to think about all this a bit," she admitted. "But I'm not leaving yet. I've got a few days left to my holiday, and I'll be staying right next door."

The telephone jangled suddenly.

"I'm sure that's Zaide," Malka's grandmother said, getting to her feet. "Finished with his morning *shiur* and wanting to know what's doing." She smiled as Mrs. Fishman answered the ring and nodded at her mother.

"See? I told you," Mrs. Meyer said. "Tell your father I'm coming straight home. I have so much to tell him." She turned to her son-in-law. "You're going out now, aren't you? Could you possibly drop me at home on the way?"

He nodded agreeably, and Mrs. Fishman went to get her mother's coat. Mrs. Meyer tucked her glasses into her handbag and followed her to the door. As she passed Judy, she stopped and gave her a quick kiss.

"Such a wonderful morning this has been," she smiled. "So much of it thanks to you. Don't worry, it isn't over. We're going to be very much in touch." She winked. "After all, we're cousins. Real ones. Fourth or fifth, twice removed, or something like that. We'll have to figure it out. Still closer than *ferd, fuss, podkeva, tshvock's an einikel!*"

She was still laughing as she went out; Judy and

## Chapter Sixteen

Malka could hear her as they stood together in the room.

"I should have known all along," Malka finally said, her voice sounding shaky from long disuse. She drew in a deep breath. "I liked you straight away, as soon as I saw you. That was the morning old Mrs. Stein was knocked down by those creatures, and you came out to help with the potatoes. Remember?"

She smiled uncertainly at Judy, suddenly shy. Judy, remembering her identical first reaction, could only nod in reply.

"We'd heard you knocking about in the house, you know," Malka admitted in sudden confession. "We called your uncle to tell him there was someone in the house and he told us not to worry."

For the second time that morning, Judy was shocked beyond words; there she had been, importantly writing about inner city dwellers who mind their own business and never get involved, while at the same time, Malka and her family were carefully watching over the house next door.

"Your uncle told us 'no problem,'" Malka continued. "'It's just my niece and a friend.'" She laughed as she quoted him. "'She's a nice Jewish girl even though she doesn't know it.'"

"He said that?" Judy gaped. Uncle Martin. She wondered. Her parents were cousins; their mothers were daughters of Great-Granny Bess. Judy vaguely remembered a long-ago Seder in Ilford with dozens of strangers around the table, identified simply as some sort of cousins, once or twice removed. Then there were weddings with brides dressed in shimmering white, and grooms decked out in top hat and tails with that rented-for-one-night look. But the only relative that they had any real relationship with was Uncle Martin and it was from him that Judy had heard those long-ago stories as he sat in their cottage kitchen, gulping his coffee along with its steam. Perhaps, those long-ago memories had indeed surfaced in her dreams, somehow fleshed out into real life figures. That would be an easy explanation of her restless nights and days on Kyverdale Road, but maybe just a little too easy and pat. It didn't begin to explain all the things Uncle Martin himself could not have known, the details, the dialogue, the thoughts and feelings of those long-lost relatives, thoughts and feelings that had become Judy's own as she relived their lives in her dreams.

She looked up as Malka laughed again. "A nice Jewish girl," she repeated. "When my mother heard that, she said we ought to invite you over. Why do you think I never even asked her permisson before I told you to come in yesterday, when you were locked out?"

She eyed her again quietly as Judy groped for something to say. Malka started to speak; she hesitated and then seemed to decide to come right out and say it.

"Judy," she said, her voice sounding faintly accusing. "You knew all along, didn't you. I watched your face. You were happy and excited like the rest of us but you weren't surprised." She paused. "Am I crazy, or am I right?"

Judy took a deep breath. "You're not crazy, Malka. You're right. I'll tell you all about it, but first you must promise not to laugh."

"I wouldn't laugh at you," Malka said seriously.

Judy nodded. "No, you wouldn't, would you. All right, then. Tell me, what do you know about — about...dreams?"

## Chapter Seventeen

Judy lay on her back in the bright orange sleeping bag, her arms underneath her head. Through the window she could see the bare tree branches bending and swaying in the winter wind, throwing shadows across the moonlit street. The room was quiet, though both girls were awake. Penny lay sprawled in her sleeping bag with her head buried in yet another mystery book from the endless supply in her backpack. Her round, placid eyes were fixed on the page before her, reading the words without trying to read between the lines. Not that there was anything between those lines, Judy knew. It was all straightforward junk that took no effort to read and left you with absolutely nothing.

Judy closed her eyes for a moment, seeing before her again the beautiful *sefer Torah* with its special *atzei chayim*. It was the centerpiece of what she had experienced during this very special day; a morning of discovery and an afternoon of disclosure, when she had finally shared with Malka her private world in the house on Kyverdale Road. Again, they had been interrupted by Penny's arrival. This time, Penny had knocked at the Fishmans' door, and seemed to accept the closeness that had obviously developed between the two girls.

The stillness circulated through the room, broken only by the faint riffle of pages. Judy looked across at Penny, a mild wave of irritation rising within her. They had been friends for so very long that they didn't need to talk much; the silences that fell between them were usually the companionable kind. But now Judy thought of the long afternoon next door, and she felt this silence stretch endlessly. Even if she'd wanted to chat, she couldn't think of a thing to say.

Judy stretched and yawned, then, settling herself more comfortably, she opened the book that Malka had lent her the day before.

"What book did she give you, Judy?" Penny peered curiously over the gray nylon of her sleeping bag. "Anything interesting?"

"Don't know yet." Judy answered, looking down at the title page. "It's some sort of history book, I think."

"History! You're joking." Penny stared. "Oh well, hope you enjoy it." And she went back to her novel. She had only ten pages left to read and she still didn't know who the murderer was.

Two chapters later, the sound of deep breathing brought Judy up from the depths of her book. Penny was sound asleep in her sleeping bag, her head pillowed on the mystery novel, as if to say: *Case closed!* Judy smiled. She was grateful to Penny for having gone off on her own today, leaving Judy alone to enjoy this special day.

She turned back to Malka's book; she found that she was actually enjoying it and she couldn't decide why. She'd always thought of history as the best cure for insomnia, but somehow this book was different. She thought of her reaction when she'd first picked it up from the table in Malka's hall; it was her own history that she

## Chapter Seventeen

was reading. She remembered the day they had gone to the Tower of London. It was then that she'd sensed the first glimmering of feeling that was growing inside her; she wasn't some brown autumn leaf that had fallen off a tree and was now flitting down the road to wherever the wind might take it. Instead, she was an actual branch of a tree that was still firmly rooted in its place; maybe a thin and delicate branch, but with real direction in which to grow.

The book that Malka had given her was taking her back to the very beginning, to the start of what Leibel and Yehudis had only continued, as links in a very long chain. She turned to the next chapter, flipping over the crisp, smooth paper, and Penny stirred in her sleep. I really should let her sleep, Judy thought. She's had a long day trudging around town.

Judy rummaged around the end of her sleeping bag, and pulled out her pale blue thermal blanket. At home near the sea, she slept with it wrapped around her, like a mummy, under her down quilt. It felt just as good here in London, wrapped around her each night, as she lay zipped up into the sleeping bag. Now, she bundled the blanket over her arm and, taking the book, she gently shut the light and tiptoed down the stairs, leaving Penny snoring quietly into the darkness. She started down the sagging steps to the kitchen and then changed her mind, turning instead towards the front of the house. The single lightbulb in the empty front room cast a friendly glow on the fresh white shades on the windows as she curled up in her blanket on the floor beside the boarded up fireplace. She opened her book and started to read Chapter Three.

It wasn't that the book was boring; she'd found it interesting from the very beginning, and as she continued to read, even more so. But it had been a very long day. Not as taxing on her legs as a day of touring in Westminster or shopping in the mall would have been, but the emotions that had raged through her so many times that day had taken their toll. She was exhausted, and she found herself nodding off over the history book.

For a moment Judy wiggled uncomfortably; she missed the wadding of her sleeping bag that usually cushioned her from the hard flat flooring, and a tiny voice still awake in her brain urged her to get back into bed. Then as her head drooped into the crook of her arm, a feeling of warmth and comfort slowly seeped through the pale blue blanket wrapped around her. Dimly she became aware of a soft velvety touch and a glowing warmth that the cranky central heating had never provided. The bare white light bulb seemed to gradually dim and seepen, casting an amber light on the page of her book. Judy looked up to see if the light bulb was going out, reaching an arm out of the folds of her covering, yet her brain could not quite comprehend what her fingers were feeling: the deep soft velvet nap of an armchair, long silky threads of a cushion fringe, and the soft fine feel of a bit of crocheted lace draped over the back of the seat. "I'm dreaming," she realized, welcoming the warm glow of the room about her.

The deep plush cushion shifted with her weight as she looked up and around, squinting with the effort to see what she could feel. Then the soft blur of the room around her became focused, as if someone was slowly turning the knob on a slide projector, and she realized what had happened. This time there was no glass barrier. The invisible wall was gone, and even in her dream, she was finally inside the front room of the house on Kyverdale Road.

## Chapter Eighteen

Judy found herself still hugging her pale blue blanket as she lay curled up on the plush wine armchair, looking for all the world like a Victorian invalid wrapped in a crocheted afghan. She hurriedly straightened up, swinging her legs out before her and rolling up the blanket behind her back, out of sight. As the room swung into focus, she could see vague familiar outlines by the door and for a moment she wondered if the barrier was back in place, with Yehudis and Leibel out in the hallway where she used to stand, while she was trapped inside. Then the misty shapes in the doorway sharpened and cleared as they stepped into the room; Judy watched as Yehudis placed her hand on the polished door handle and firmly pushed the door shut.

The armchair was deep and soft, and, screened by the folds of the starched white cloth that had not yet been removed from the table, Judy felt like an intruder trying to hide from sight. The brass candlesticks still stood at the center, with fresh candles flickering inside them, but somehow these tall white waxen spears seemed like imposters, trying to imitate the glow of the Friday night flames. The peace that had radiated from the Shabbos candles was gone, and in its place was a tension that charged the air and hung like a cloud above Yehudis and

*Leibel as they faced each other before the closed door.*

"*I showed her I wasn't too pleased, and she's gone up to change.*" *Yehudis spoke softly, but her voice was not gentle. It was the hard and hushed tone of someone afraid that her words would be overheard.*

*Leibel's back was to Judy. She could not hear his reply but she could see the dispirited droop of his head, the flecks of gray in his hair, the unfamilair slope of his shoulders. He seemed to have aged years overnight and she wondered why.*

*For a moment, Yehudis stood ramrod straight, her dark eyes flashing; she looked as Judy had never seen her. Then she softened, and when she spoke, her voice was a strange blend of sorrow and resignation, with a faint pulse of anger throbbing behind it.*

"*You've given up, Leibel. Haven't you?*" *The thinly etched lines on her clear sweet face seemed to deepen as she spoke.* "*You've thrown up your hands to those cynics on the shul committee and you just stay out of their way. And here in this house, you hide yourself in your Gemara and you leave me to do the fighting.*"

*Judy watched the broad shoulders heave in a tired sigh as Leibel shrugged in resignation.* "*You can fight Russian peasants, Yehudis. Or at least, you can try to. But you can't fight modern progress in these Western countries.*"

"*No?*"

"*No.*" *he said sadly.* "*Look at that silly law they've had on the books for these past thirty years. It's true that those first motor cars made an awful noise and scared everyone out of their wits. When they came down the road, the horses bolted in every direction. So they tried to stop it all by making new laws: every horseless carriage has to have a man walk before it, carrying a big red flag.*" *He laughed shortly.*

## Chapter Eighteen

"Silly people. They'll have to face facts soon; these motor cars are here to stay. They're being improved and perfected each year, and there's no way they'll keep them off the road much longer. Soon they'll get rid of that Red Flag law and eventually, the horses will all go back to the farm. See what I mean? You just can't fight progress."

"No. I don't see what you mean, Leibel." Yehudis said evenly. "And I'm sure you don't really mean it either. I'll tell you something, Leibel. You're right. The streets will one day be full of motor cars. But I'll tell you something else," she continued. "One day, those motor cars will be driven by bearded young men like you, who are off to their daily evening shiur or perhaps to daven minchah."

Her voice rose in tone, even though she took care to keep its volume low. "Leibel, who says progress means moving forward with empty hands? Why do we have to leave behind everything that's important?"

Her clear words echoed through the quiet room as the fire crackled its approval. Leibel bent his head, remembering the words he had spoken to Itche in the little village in the Ukraine.

Yehudis spoke gently as she shared his thoughts. Itche. The very thought of his name gnawed at them like a burning ulcer. "Have you spoken recently with Itche?"

Leibel sighed. "I don't see him much these days. My office is on the ground floor where I can speak to the people unloading the crates. His is somewhere on the third floor, in a carpeted room with electric lighting, and a prim young secretary to guard his door. He's come a long way from the simple villager who chewed a straw as he walked through the marketplace. His cousin left him the business and he feels it's not his fault that the place just about runs itself, in exactly the way his cousin ran it for years."

"On Shabbos and Yom Tov."

"Yes." His voice was barely audible. "So he comes in on Shabbos. And Yom Tov. He walks the miles there after kiddush, just to make sure everything is running smoothly. Or so he says. And he won't force me to come in when I don't want to. He doesn't even make me come in on Chol Ha-moed. He has a good memory and he's still grateful to me for a lot of things."

He paused.

"But he's beginning to stay out of my way. He doesn't like some of the things that I say to him when we do bump into each other. So he stays in his office and I stay in mine."

"And everything's fine?"

"No." Leibel's shoulders sagged as he spoke. "Everything's far from fine. You know, Yehudis," he turned to her sadly. "I never even told you this. The very first year that we lived here, after the move from the East End, it was Yom Kippur night and Chaya'le was too young to walk all the way to Lordship Park and back in the dark. Do you remember? You stayed home and I was on my way home alone, after davening. Suddenly, from down the still, dark street, I could hear a quiet niggun. Imagine it. There in the elegant roads of Stamford Hill, I could clearly hear someone singing the Kol Nidrei."

He stopped for a moment remembering, and then he continued. "Would you believe it, Yehudis? I looked all around me, but there wasn't a soul on the street. And then I saw it. A horse-drawn cart was rumbling down the road behind me, driven by a small stout man wearing a soft cloth cap. As the wagon drove past me, the niggun lingered behind it and I realized that it was the driver who was singing the Kol Nidrei as he drove his horse home from work. He sang it sadly as if to say, 'Hashem, please help me, because I can't help myself.'"

## Chapter Eighteen

Leibel looked up with a sudden motion, more in fear than in anger. "And that was the first time I wondered if we would have been better off back in the Ukraine."

Or the East End.

The unspoken words shouted between them but Yehudis was silent; there wasn't much that she could say. Then a soft step sounded down the staircase and she quickly opened the door.

"Chaya'le?"

Judy blinked as a smart young woman came through the door and then she understood. The smell of spices that still hovered over the room had signaled the end of Shabbos, but it was not the Shabbos that she had seen two nights before. Years had passed and the thick glossy curls on the child she remembered were pulled back in a twist at the nape of her neck. A bright silk tie swung elegantly from the high collar of her crisp lace blouse, down to the gold buckle at the waist of her long slim skirt. She carried a straw boater in her hand, which she placed lightly on her head as she entered and, striding purposefully over to the mirror, she arranged a long net scarf casually over it, draping the netting carefully over her face. Judy cowered in the armchair, trying to disappear into its depths, but she needn't have worried; the young adult that Chaya'le had grown into only had eyes for herself in the mirror above the mantlepiece.

Leibel cleared his throat. "Why over the face, Chaya'le?" he smiled with a falsely jocular air.

Chaya'le patiently answered his reflection in the mirror as she adjusted the folds of the net. "The rubber wheels stir up clouds of dust in the street, Papa. Everyone wears these."

"Even the men?"

"Oh, Papa. The men wear goggles. And capes."

*She pulled on a pair of kid gloves and gave her hair one last satisfied pat.*

"And who is taking you?" Her mother's usually gentle voice had a short sharp edge to it that she seemed to be trying to swallow.

Chaya'le stopped short. "Victor got permission from his father to use the motorcar," she said quietly, forcing her voice to stay calm. "He's taking Mary and Jennifer. And me."

"And who is Victor?" Leibel's voice, too, sounded suddenly tense.

"Victor is Jennifer's married brother. Mary is his wife, if you must know." The clear young voice sharpened. "And what's so terrible about all that?"

"Nothing at all," Leibel said hastily.

Yehudis was silent. She opened her mouth, then thought better of it and closed it again, as if counting each syllable carefully before letting it sound in the room. "And where are you going?" she finally asked.

"Oh, just to a small cafe down in Tottenham," Chaya'le said lightly. "The road in that direction is easy on the motorcar. We won't be going very far. Does that set your mind at ease?"

"And what will you eat there?"

Chaya'le's mouth was a grim straight line in her face as she answered. "You've fed me very well all Shabbos, Mama. I'm not exactly hungry. Maybe I'll have a glass of lemonade, just to keep them company."

She turned to her mother, her veil moving sharply as she spoke. "Or is that also not allowed now?"

"Chaya'le..." Leibel tried to intervene as he heard her voice grow shrill.

The slim young figure moved swiftly towards the door and she paused with her hand on the door knob. A patch of

## Chapter Eighteen

red burned on each cheekbone beneath the black netting, and her voice shook. "I've had enough, Mama. It's not Shabbos, now. We've made havdalah, haven't we? I can't go out on Shabbos, and I can't go out after Shabbos without a full scale interrogation. This place is just one big prison and I'm getting out!"

A gust of wind blew in through the doorway as she pulled the front door open with a sudden angry jerk, slamming it shut behind her. The candles on the table flickered and went out.

The sputtering sound of an oncoming motorcar echoed through the quiet room. Leibel stood stiff with shock, still staring out at the hallway, as if hoping that Chaya'le would relent and return. Judy watched as Yehudis just stood, her slender shoulders sagging, as if melting away into the thin trail of tears that began to trickle slowly down her cheeks.

"Leibel," she said quietly, a catch in her voice. "My father blessed us with shalom, with peace. But sometimes I wonder if too much peace is a very good thing."

Leibel opened his mouth as if to reply, to remonstrate with her, to shout that it isn't true. But then he closed it in a stiff straight line that began to waver beneath his beard. The drops that coursed down Yehudis' cheeks turned into a stream as the motorcar sounded closer, and sobs shook her small slight frame.

"Forgive my weakness, Leibel," she choked, fumbling for her handkerchief in the sleeve of her thick dark dress. "I try not to cry. But it's hard. The tears overflow on their own."

"I'm afraid that I've been the weak one, Yehudis." Leibel's voice was rough as he strained to steady it before he continued. "But I don't think you should keep back those tears. Let them come. Tears are never wasted. Let

*Hashem see them. Those tears have the power to float your tefillos right past all the barriers, straight to His throne."* He swallowed.

*"Perhaps your tears won't help Chaya'le," he said. "Or at least they won't do more than prevent her from straying too far. But Hashem will remember every tear that you shed. He will collect them all and save them. And your tefillos that have been saved along with them, will help our grandchildren. And theirs that follow, wherever they'll wander to. He will give them the* siyata d'Shemaya *to keep to His path, until Mashiach will come to take us all home."*

*The motorcar rattled to a halt in front of the house, and they could hear light, hurried footsteps approach it as voices called out in welcome. Yehudis reached for the small thick volume that lay on the table in the corner and her husband came to stand by her side near the window. They pushed aside the heavy lace curtains, and from her seat on the armchair, Judy could see the vague black shadow of the motorcar shimmering in the darkness of the street, an occasional amber gleam of the streetlamp glancing off its polished chrome panels.*

*The slim young figure climbed onto the step, and reached out to the helping hands which held the door open. Her black net scarf blew out behind her, and Judy blinked. The deep yellow glow from the streetlight danced in the shadowy night, playing tricks on her vision and, for a moment, she saw a small slim figure in jeans with a bright orange backpack behind, climb into the car as it moved away. She looked down at herself, as if to make sure that she was still there, and she saw, in place of the faded nightshirt she'd been wearing, the woolen top and the pleated skirt she'd borrowed from Malka, which she'd returned the day before. Then she heard Leibel's voice as he spoke in the stillness; it sounded different from the way*

## Chapter Eighteen

*it had just a moment ago, with more of his old fire and strength.* "You carry on in just that direction, Yehudis," he said clearly. "And we'll be behind you."

We'll be behind you.

*Judy looked up in confusion and realized that Leibel was speaking to her. Yehudis, he called her. Well, that was her name. The white lace cutains swung gently behind him as he stood with his wife by the window. They were no longer looking out at the departing lights of the sputtering motorcar, but had turned to the plush wine armchair where Judy still sat. This time, she knew they could see her, and she found herself smiling uncertainly to them as they gazed directly at her, smiling gently in return. It seemed so natural.*

We'll be behind you.

The words hovered gently in the air, along with the fragrance of spices and the faint scent of pine, as Judy watched the scene before her slowly blur and fade and she knew with a sudden certainty that she would never see them again. She felt herself reach out her hands, as if to grab onto the armchair and table, and keep them from dissolving like blocks of ice in the sun, but her fingers groped about in the empty air.

The room grew cold but the glow of the smiling faces remained, warming her through the thin blue blanket that was wrapped around her as she lay in her nightshirt on the bare wooden floorboards. Judy reached out to the floor beside her and picked up the square white book, the only object that filled a space in the large bare room. She wished that Yehudis and Leibel had left her with something, at least the small thick volume that Yehudis had held so carefully, so fondly, every time that she'd seen her. Yet she knew that Malka would find her one just like it, and teach her to read it and recite the words that were written inside.

A door banged upstairs suddenly and Judy jumped; her collision with the mantlepiece brought her back down to earth. Then she heard a quiet voice calling, "Judy? Are you there?"

CHAPTER NINETEEN

"Judy?"

Penny's voice was louder this time, a faint note of panic creeping inside it as she called from the upstairs landing.

Judy came to life, padding over to the front room doorway and poking her head out into the hall. "I'm here, Penny," she said calmly. "Sorry to frighten you. I didn't want to disturb you so I came downstairs to read."

"Oh." Penny sighed in relief as she came down the steps two at a time. "You know, it's funny. It's been just the two of us in this big empty house but it's never been creepy. Waking up now and finding you gone was the first time I ever felt scared."

She looked around the empty room. "Funny place to make yourself comfy, Judy." Then she sniffed. "You been cleaning or something?"

"Cleaning?" Judy echoed.

Penny sniffed the air again, like a small worried puppy. "Sorry. My mistake. It smelled like pine for a minute."

Judy stared for a moment, then shrugged her shoulders, "Well, you did insist on drowning this place in Rough Tough." But she found herself looking around the room uneasily, as if trying to see if there were any traces left from the warm furnished room that she had seen there only minutes before. Penny followed her gaze and then turned a worried face to Judy.

"Are you alright, Judy?" she said. "You know, I've been wondering if I should drag you home to your Mum. You've been acting awfully funny since we've arrived here, and you're only getting worse."

Judy did not know what to answer. But she knew that things were going to be very different now, and she owed Penny some explanation. If not for Penny agreeing to keep her company, she could never have come to the house on Kyverdale Road. "Penny," she said hesitantly. "Why don't we go into the kitchen for a cup of tea. And I'll tell you all about it."

Half an hour later, Penny reached out for the glass before her on the rickety kitchen table. She sipped the stone cold tea and made a face, then stood up to put the kettle back on the stove. She found herself taking comfort in these small ordinary actions, avoiding Judy's glance as she sat by the table, spent with the story she'd told.

The kettle started to boil, filling the kitchen with a friendly cloud of steam, and Penny poured out two fresh cups of tea. Sitting back down on the little stool, she nursed the hot tea between her cupped hands, staring reflectively into its depths.

"You know, Judy," she finally said. "Your dreams. It's almost as if they're calling you." The metal teaspoon clinked as she stirred in a spoonful of sugar. "It's funny," she continued. "The furthest back I can go is to my Great-Grandma Martha. She was in service in the manor house a few miles from Chichester, working her way up from housemaid to house keeper for some bigwig; I don't remember his name. She married the third footman, I think it was, and the Earl, or whatever title they called him, gave

## Chapter Nineteen

them a cottage with a scrap of garden for their wedding. Generous fellow, wasn't he? My grandfather still runs a market garden. Been weeding since he could walk." She laughed. "My father's side I really don't know, and I don't think I'll try to find out. Imagine what it would be like going all the way back. With my strawberry blonde hair, I'd probably discover some Celtic serf running around in a fur skin somewhere near Stonehenge!"

Judy smiled into her tea. The warm drink felt good as it went down her throat; it was dry from all the talking she'd done. In a strange way, sharing her dreams with Penny had been easy; it was just a matter of telling a fascinating story and knowing that Penny, who knew her since she was born, would believe it. With Malka, the decision to share had been so much harder; as she related her dream in detail, she could feel every word she said echo through the room in a silent shout: *And what are you going to do about all this?* The decision to share it with Malka had really been a decision for so much more.

Penny eyed Judy from over her steaming glass. "You know, Judy," she said quietly, "you always were different from all the rest of us. Oh, not in an obvious way," she hastened to add. "It's just that there was a certain something that seemed to drive you along. A sort of restlessness that made you keep looking to see what was around the next corner."

"Did you really feel that?" Judy wondered. "Sometimes I thought I was imagining it. There you all were, floating comfortably along, and I was feeling like someone who'd lost something and kept climbing around to find it." She thought of her plans for next year and she grinned wryly. "I thought I was just a shade more ambitious, or pushy, like my mother would say. Or nosy. But now I'm pretty sure I know what it is."

She looked anxiously at Penny, hoping she understood without trying to probe deeper. She could describe every scene to its minutest detail, making Penny see the pattern on the front room carpet, the sand on the floor of the hut in the Ukraine. But there was no way she could explain to her the peace that had radiated out of the Shabbos candles, the love that flowed from the people in the shul to the *sefer Torah* and back again, as it was held high above their heads for everyone to see. How could she tell Penny, without hurting her, that she felt closer to someone she'd met just a few days before than to someone she'd known all her life? Could she ever understand that as Judy stood before the *sefer Torah*, in the dining room of Malka's house, she'd felt like she'd finally come home?

Penny might understand the pull of the generations behind her, but only in the way that they'd pored through Bill's find in the loft; a fascination for things of long ago. A collection of coins, a pile of ancient account books, a heap of old papers; all of them equally worthless. There had been no rejoicing that they had been found, any more than the stamps that had been cut off for some long-ago schoolboy's collection, had been missed.

But Malka had understood. She had felt the thrill of the voice sounding down through the ages, and had sat frozen as Judy described each member of the family, *her* family, in detail. But she knew that what they were left with was so very much more.

"The feeling of that front room..." Malka had mused. She remembered an incident her uncle had told them when he returned from a business trip one day, several months ago. He had stayed in a hotel which was owned by someone he knew and his room was spacious and comfortable. There was something else about the room that he liked but he couldn't quite put a finger on what

## Chapter Nineteen

it was. Until it came to him, late one night, as he lay in bed, trying to fall asleep. He had spent the evening in a very satisfying way; learning in depth and with pleasure that he rarely felt, even while he sat at his daily *shiur*. He thought of the way he had *davened* that morning; the only shul in the town was far away and their minyan started too late for him to see to his various appointments. So he had *davened* in his hotel room, again with a depth and with pleasure that he would normally associate with Yom Kippur in shul. He wondered. And the next morning, he asked his friend. "Tell me, there is a very special atmosphere in the room you have given me. What is the secret of that room?"

The hotel owner had smiled. "Interesting that you should feel it," he commented. "For the past three months that room has been occupied by a young man who had come to town for medical reasons; there is a famous clinic just three minutes away from the hotel. He went there for regular treatment, a time-consuming affair. But the hours that were left to him each day, he used for what he does best; I could hear the quiet tune of his learning day and night."

"And my uncle felt it," Malka had continued. "The walls of that room had soaked up the words of the Torah and had transmitted them to the next one who came there, when he tuned in to the very same station."

Judy remembered the well worn *sefer* that lay before Leibel on the roll-top desk, and the thick little book that Yehudis had held in her hand. And she understood. The lines of transmission might have been broken over the years, but now she was receiving the message loud and clear.

She thought of the candles that occasionally flickered on her Friday night table, back at home. Her mother lit them almost as an afterthought, not thinking much about what she was doing. The woman didn't realize that she was holding onto something that she didn't want to let go of, and it was up to Judy to show her exactly what that was. She looked around the little kitchen regretfully. Soon she would be going back home, and when she'd come back to this area, as she knew she would, it wouldn't be to this house. Uncle Martin would have it renovated, probably partition it into two tiny flats where young couples who were born and bred in this borough would live, with never a thought as to who lived here a hundred years before.

Penny absently ran her finger along the rim of the empty glass, as Judy continued.

"It's strange," she said thoughtfully, swivelling her glass around as she spoke. "It may be this house that is calling me, as you put it, but it's the house next door that has really made the most noise."

"What on earth do you mean?"

"I'm not really sure," Judy said wonderingly. "But it was always something from next door. Those first two dreams came after I'd heard the chairs moving behind that dividing wall, as they set up for those lectures. Friday night, I only heard singing, but still, it was sounds from next door. The night it was quiet, I went downstairs, but there was only some fellow who was trying to climb into the broken window."

"Sounds like acid rain," Penny grinned.

Judy blinked. "What's that?"

"You know. Someone puffs some leaded gas out of his petrol tank and three miles away, a tree dies."

"Well, not quite," Judy replied. "Somehow I think this kind of rain won't do me any harm."

Penny shrugged. "Well, if you say so. What type of

## Chapter Nineteen

lectures are they always having there anyway?"

"I really don't know," Judy answered. "But there's only one way to find out."

She picked up the small paper cup that stood on the counter and laughed. "I'll have to borrow a cup of sugar."

"Oh, you won't have to do that, Judy," Penny said dryly. "Now that you're cousins, you can just invite yourself over any time." Then she added thoughtfully, "But you wouldn't know about that, would you. Until now, you haven't had much family to speak of."

## Epilogue

The sounds of the street grew suddenly hushed as music played in the distance.

"They're coming!" Malka poked Judy and Judy nudged her mother in turn, as they looked down the street into the deepening darkness. Tiny flames flickered in long rows, like headlights during rush hour. The lights grew in size as they came closer and now she could see dozens of small boys, carefully holding burning torches as they marched in a proud parade. A small open-backed truck traveled behind the marchers and from inside came the sounds that were echoing through the evening air; a three-man band, playing with joy that impelled the music out and around them.

The road was black with shadows, yet alight with joy as dark shapes danced toward them, men and boys who sang and clapped along with the music, as they backed their way up the road. Their faces were turned towards the velvet canopy that followed. It was borne aloft by four wooden poles and it struggled to contain the small crowds of men that danced within its four corners.

Judy felt an unfamiliar lump rise up in her throat as the canopy came into view. Malka's father was tall, much taller than the men who surrounded him beneath the fringed velvet square, taller even than *her* father who walked close behind. Judy could see Rabbi Fishman's arms lovingly surround the burden he held, his eyes closed with feeling as he made his way forward, directed by the surging energy of the crowd. Prickles of tears nipped at her eyelids; the *sefer Torah* was finally on its way home.

As the procession approached the brightly lit shul, new voices joined in the gathering darkness. The double front doors of the building were thrown open and several men emerged, each with a *sefer Torah* in his arms. The crowd parted to make way as the two groups danced toward each other; the old *sifrei Torah* had come to greet the new arrival.

In the darkening streets, Judy watched as the *sifrei Torah* shone their greeting; their silver crowns and breastplates reflected the light of the countless white bulbs that bedecked the welcoming shul. As if in answer, the burnished wood of the beautiful *atzei chayim* warmly glowed in return, their sculpted carvings deepening in the gloom, like character lines on a beloved face. This was no newborn *sefer Torah*, its ink barely dry on the parchment, but a living survivor, now joyously coming home.

Judy studied the crowd that danced down the street before her. There were men with hats of all shapes and sizes, joined together by the joy of the moment. She could see the occasional bareheaded man in the crowd, drawn there by curiosity or the need to belong and she thought of all the leaves that had blown away from the tree. Maybe somewhere in this crowd stood a grandson of Itche, bewildered by what he was seeing, with no idea of how to join, or if he even wanted to. The words *siyata d'Shemaya* rang through her head as she tucked her hand into the crook of her mother's elbow and thought

## Epilogue

of the chain of events that had brought them so far. They flashed through her mind like the disjointed screenplay she'd seen that day as she stood in the doorway on Kyverdale Road. Then it had been horses and carriages and old-fashioned steamships, and now it was ordinary school projects that brought her to London, and modern-day airplanes that had brought the *sefer Torah* out of Lvov. But one thing had followed the other in orderly succession, bringing her up to where she stood now. Like the century-old *sefer Torah*, she was not an alien newcomer, but a living survivor who was finally coming back home.

She turned to meet Malka's gaze and they smiled at each other. She could feel her presence beside her, along with the warmth that flowed from the two older women at Malka's side. Judy smiled as her mother nodded her head to something Mrs. Fishman whispered; her occasional words of explanation guided Mrs. Marks throughout as she tried to absorb the new sights and sounds that surrounded her. Judy thought of the Shabbos her family had spent in the Fishman house and she smiled again. The new arrivals had been made to feel so very welcome.

By now, the procession had reached the front of the shul and the crowd was beginning to disperse. The two groups had merged together, and the *sifrei Torah* were being brought up the stairs, new and old joined as they went through the door. Judy followed the crowd of women who made their way to the gallery, where the sights and sounds of the joyous dancing below swirled about them, encompassing all with warmth and emotion, as the scrolls were brought back to the waiting *aron kodesh*.

Malka looked at her watch and turned to the others; as if by common consent they started down the steps. It was time to set up for the festive meal that would follow tonight. As they reached the cold of the street, Judy still felt the pull of the music and stood in her place, absorbing the light that shone from the shul. She remembered the two pinpricks of light that had emerged from the rushing figures in her dream, and the peace that had radiated from them when they finally found their place, back on the Shabbos table.

*V'yasem l'cha shalom,* Reb Simcha the *Kohen* had blessed his children. She could feel the first glimmering of peace spreading its rays within her as she stood there at that moment. Then, taking one last look at the brightly lit shul, she turned to catch up with the others, and they made their way back home to Kyverdale Road.

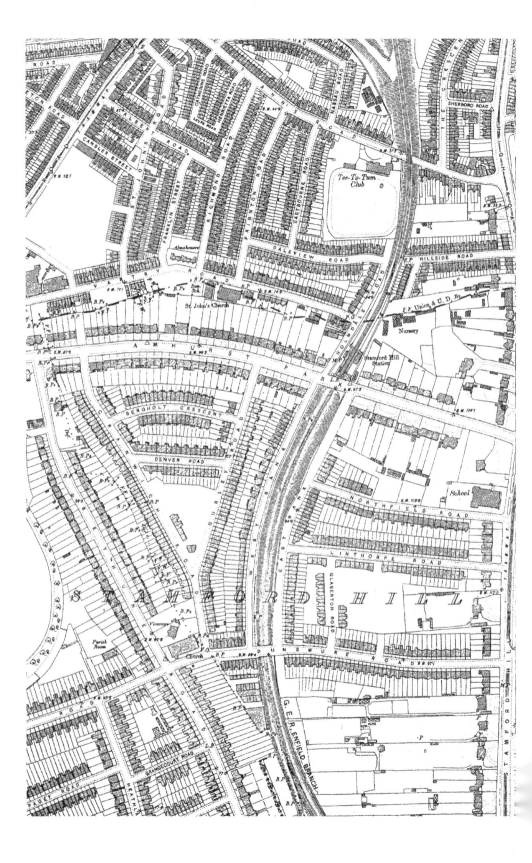

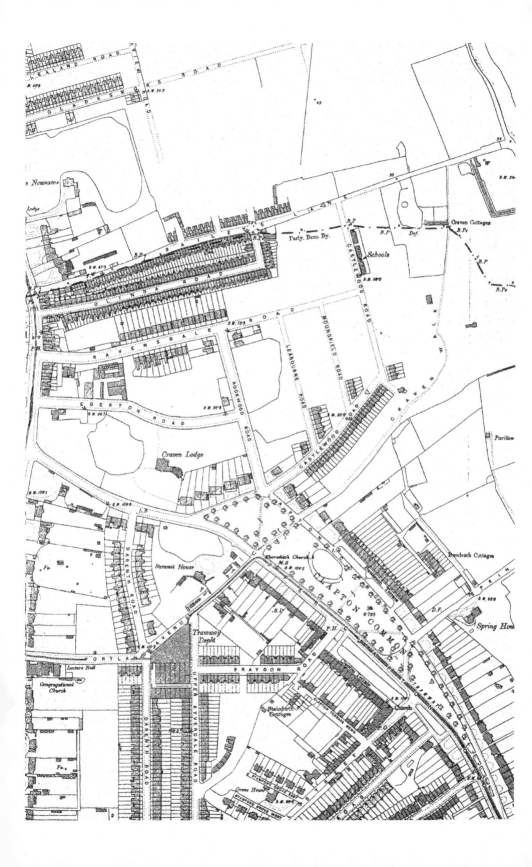

Made in the USA
Monee, IL
02 August 2023

40307724R00132